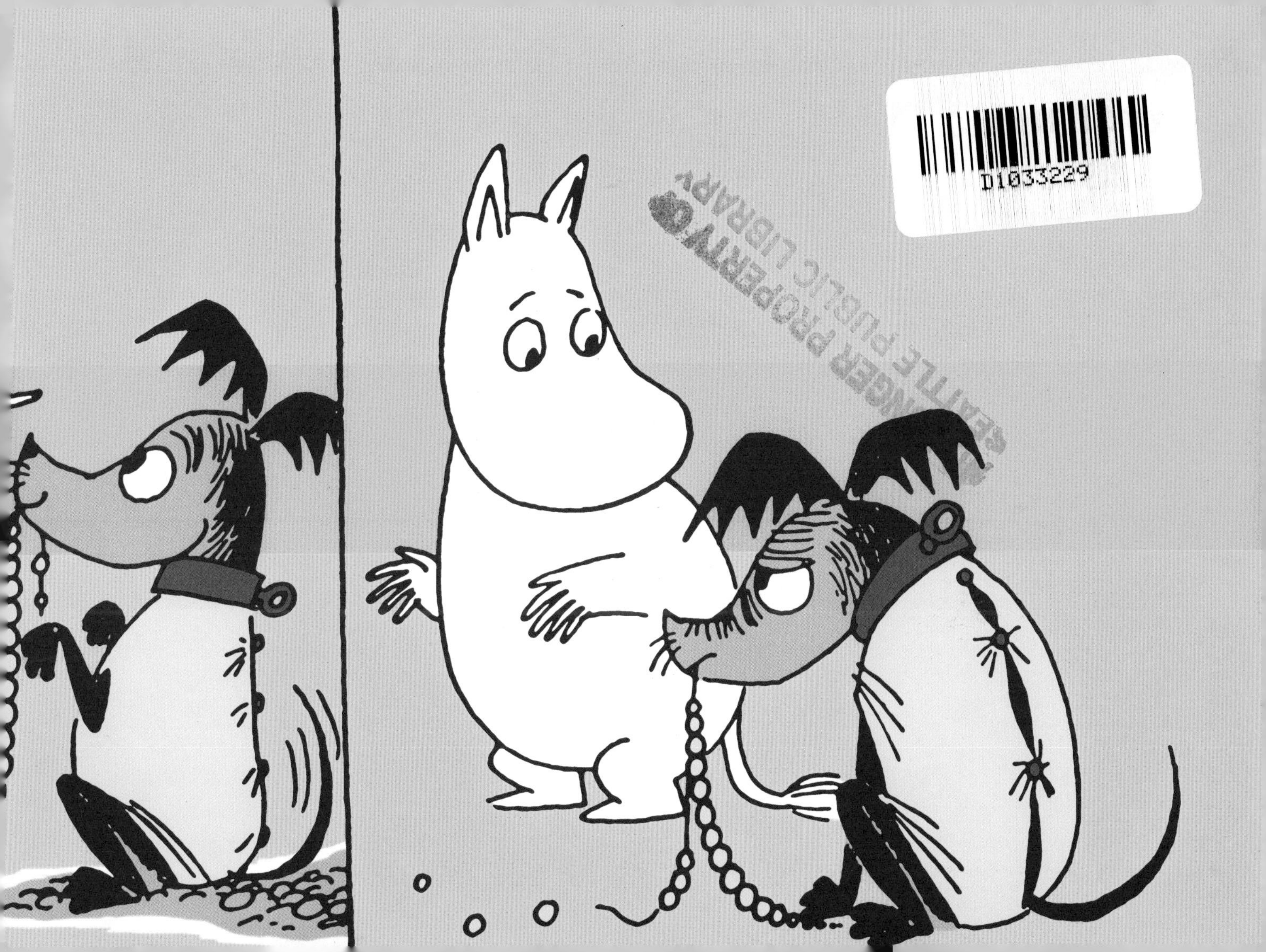

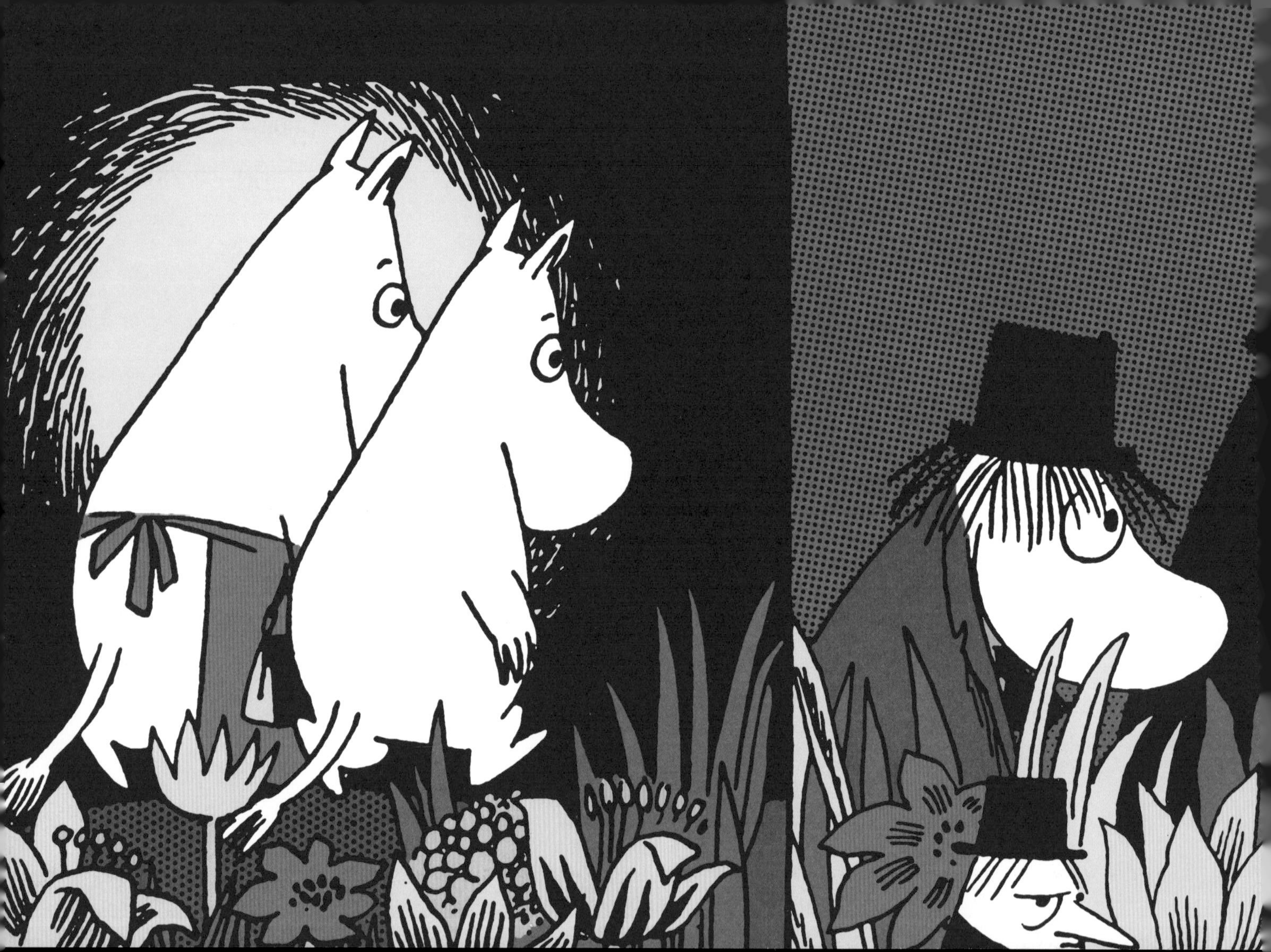

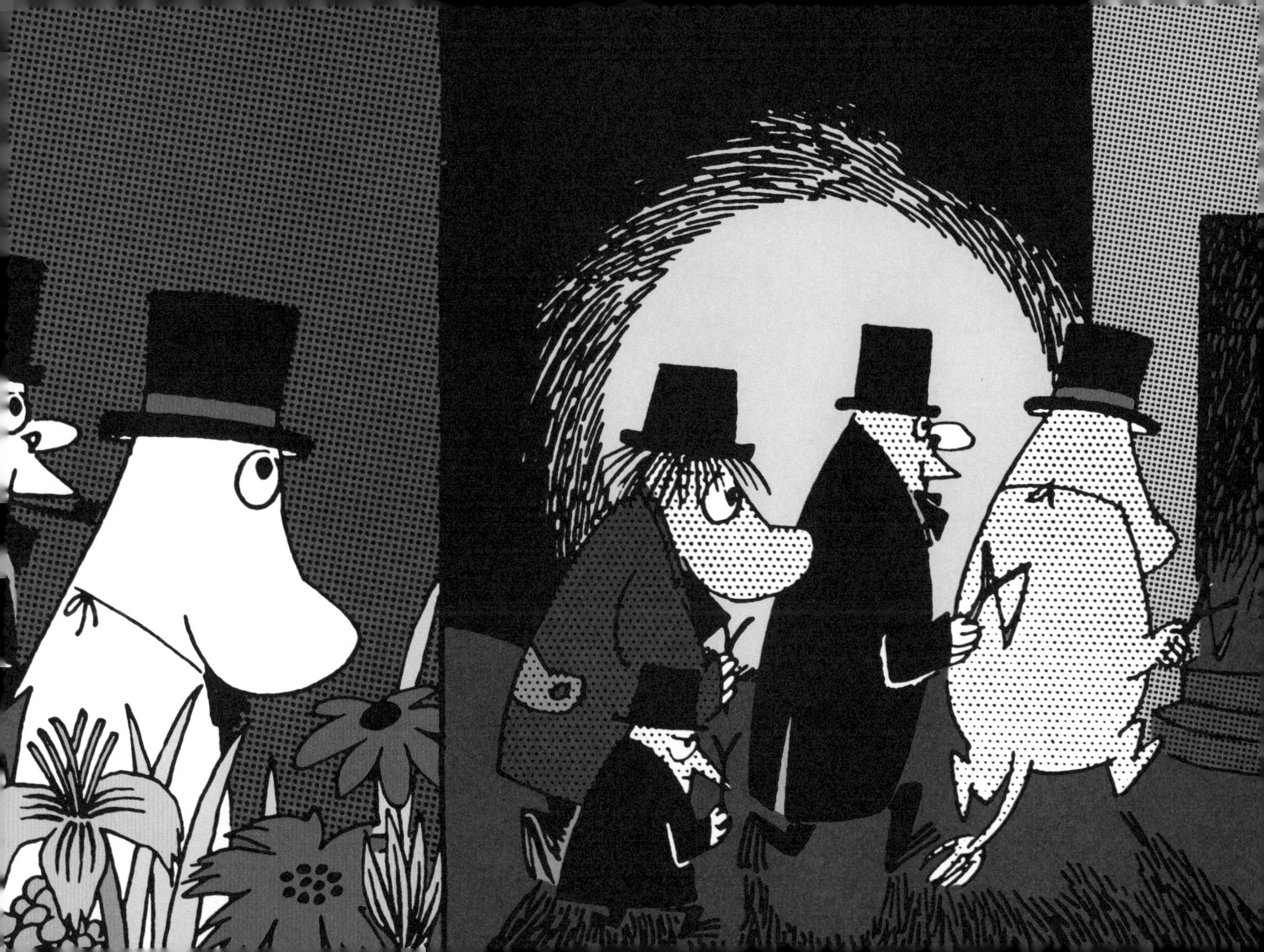

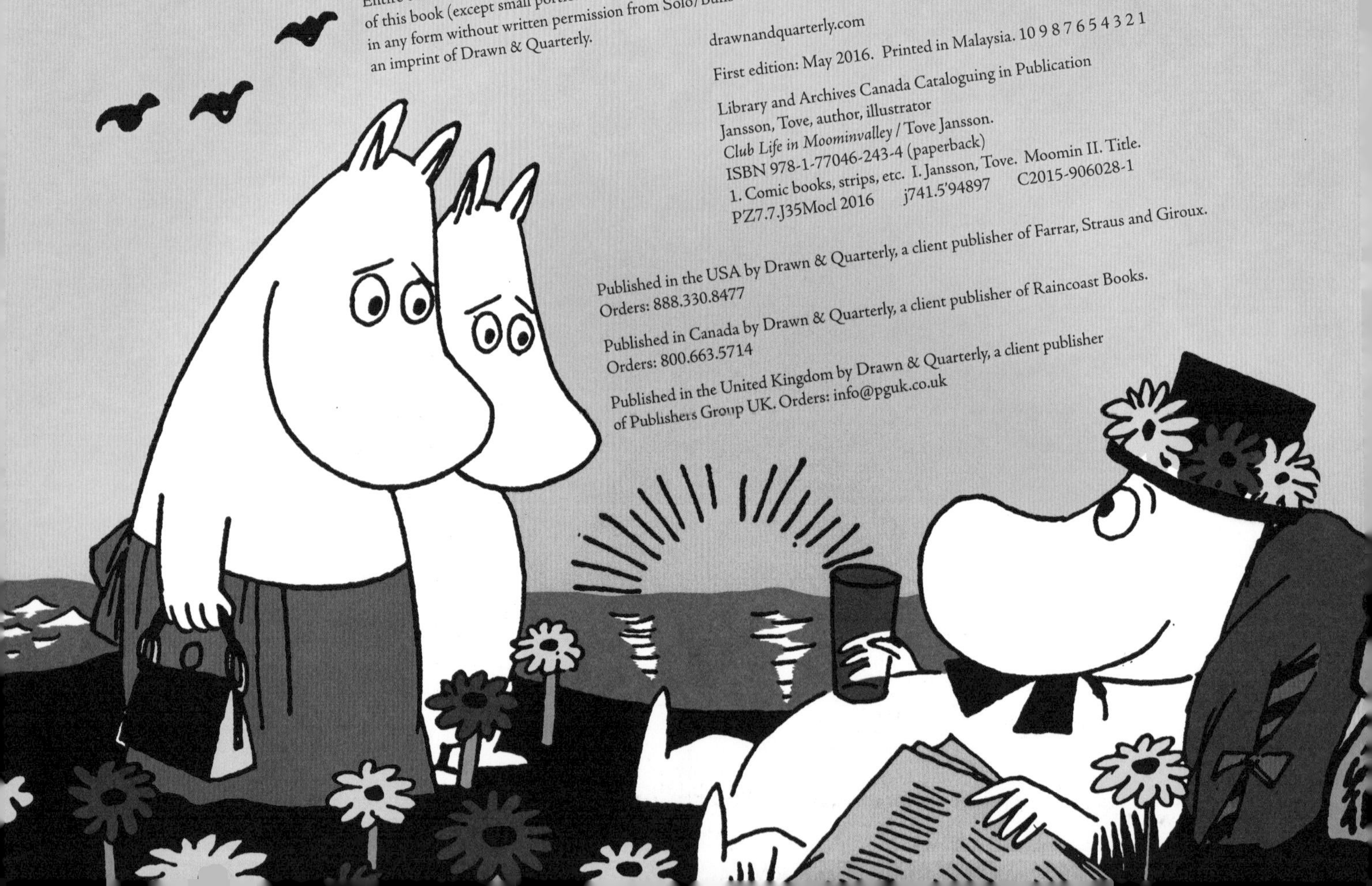

drawnandquarterly.com

First edition: May 2016. Printed in Malaysia. 10 9 8 7 6 5 4 3 2 1

Library and Archives Canada Cataloguing in Publication
Jansson, Tove, author, illustrator
Club Life in Moominvalley / Tove Jansson.
ISBN 978-1-77046-243-4 (paperback)
1. Comic books, strips, etc. I. Jansson, Tove. Moomin II. Title.
PZ7.7.J35Mocl 2016 j741.5'94897 C2015-906028-1

Published in the USA by Drawn & Quarterly, a client publisher of Farrar, Straus and Giroux.
Orders: 888.330.8477

Published in Canada by Drawn & Quarterly, a client publisher of Raincoast Books.
Orders: 800.663.5714

Published in the United Kingdom by Drawn & Quarterly, a client publisher of Publishers Group UK. Orders: info@pguk.co.uk

CLUB LIFE IN MOOMIN VALLEY

Tove Jansson

ENFANT

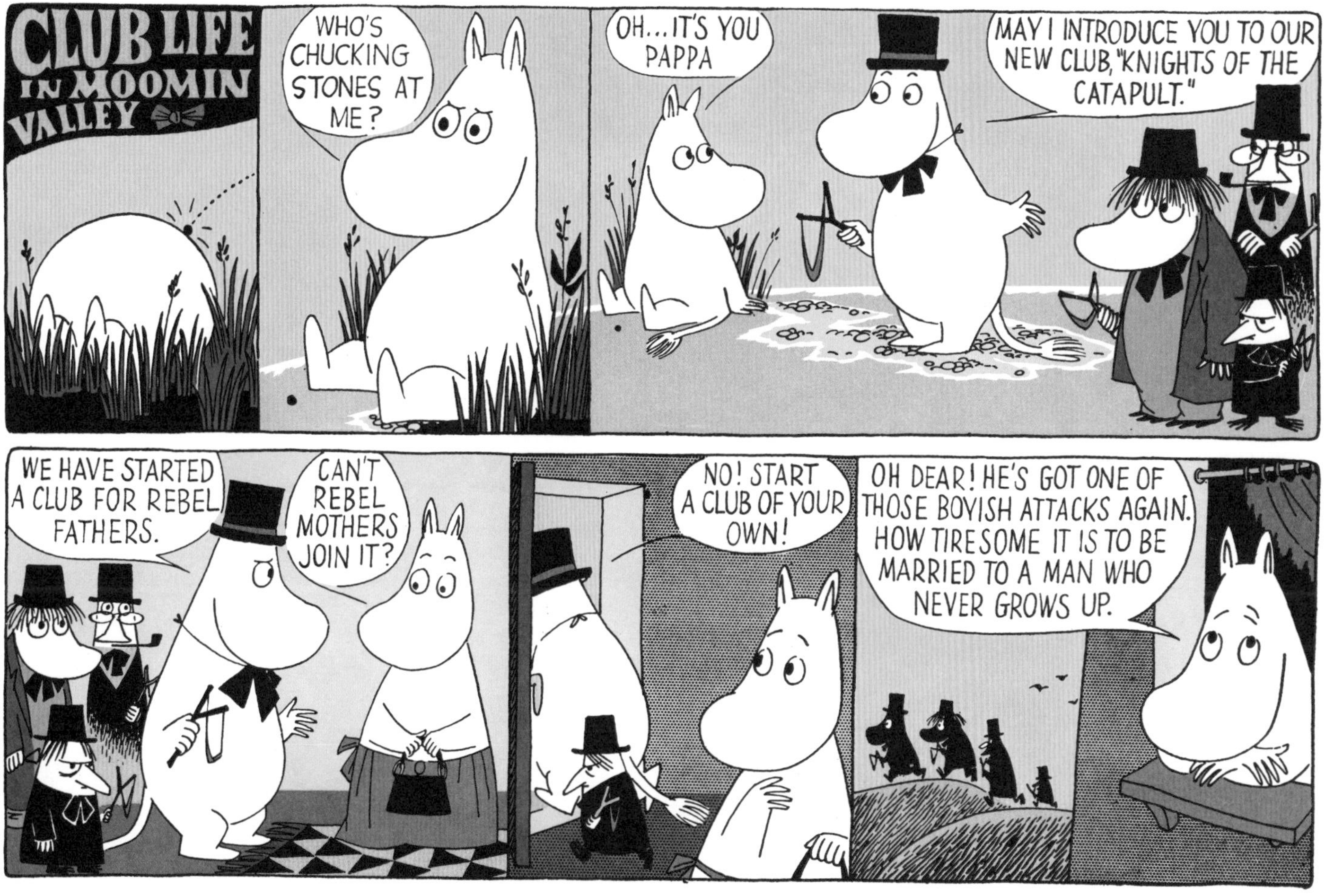
CLUB LIFE IN MOOMIN VALLEY
WHO'S CHUCKING STONES AT ME?
OH... IT'S YOU PAPPA
MAY I INTRODUCE YOU TO OUR NEW CLUB, "KNIGHTS OF THE CATAPULT."
WE HAVE STARTED A CLUB FOR REBEL FATHERS.
CAN'T REBEL MOTHERS JOIN IT?
NO! START A CLUB OF YOUR OWN!
OH DEAR! HE'S GOT ONE OF THOSE BOYISH ATTACKS AGAIN. HOW TIRESOME IT IS TO BE MARRIED TO A MAN WHO NEVER GROWS UP.

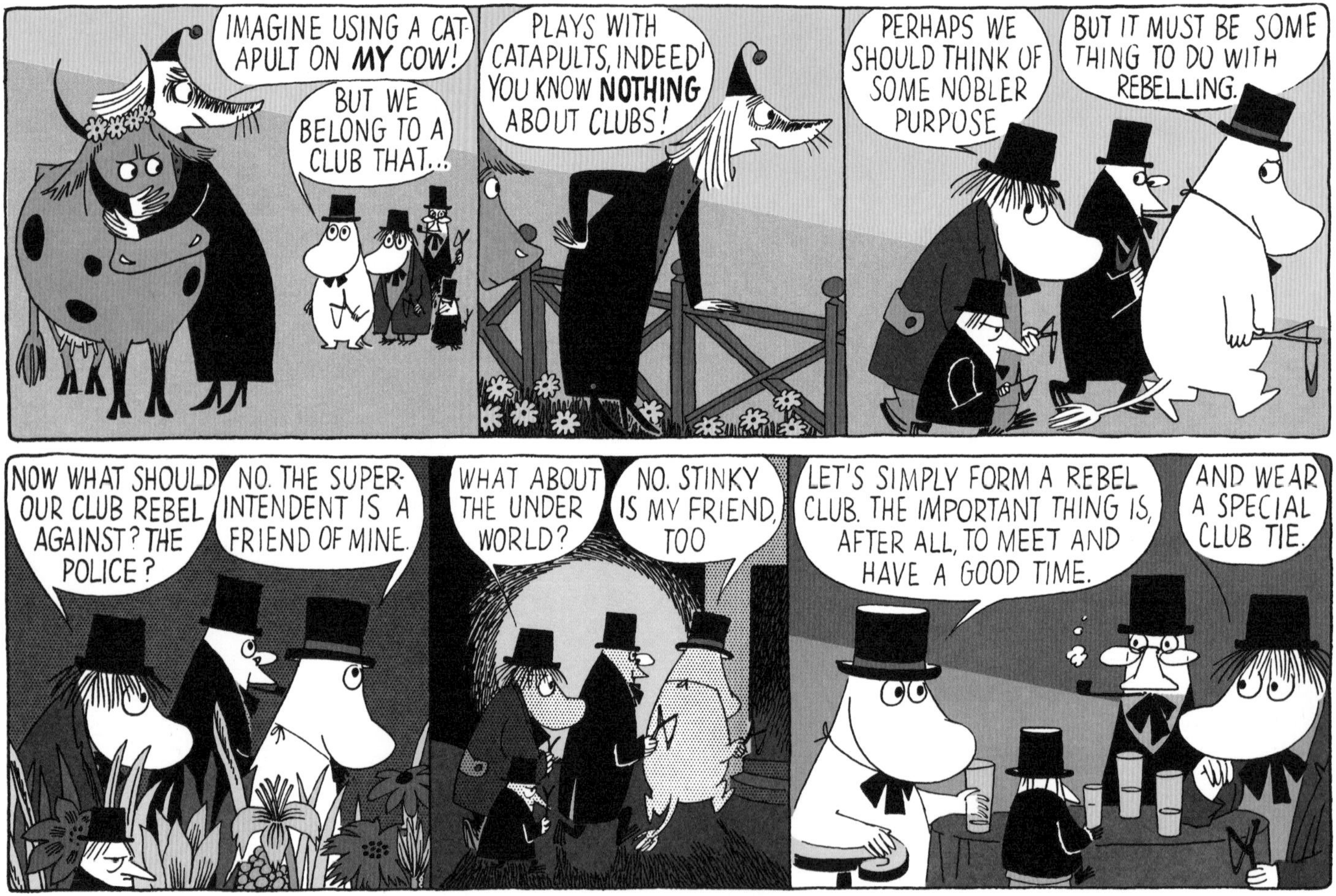
IMAGINE USING A CAT-APULT ON **MY** COW!
BUT WE BELONG TO A CLUB THAT...
PLAYS WITH CATAPULTS, INDEED! YOU KNOW **NOTHING** ABOUT CLUBS!
PERHAPS WE SHOULD THINK OF SOME NOBLER PURPOSE
BUT IT MUST BE SOME THING TO DO WITH REBELLING.
NOW WHAT SHOULD OUR CLUB REBEL AGAINST? THE POLICE?
NO. THE SUPER-INTENDENT IS A FRIEND OF MINE.
WHAT ABOUT THE UNDER WORLD?
NO. STINKY IS MY FRIEND, TOO
LET'S SIMPLY FORM A REBEL CLUB. THE IMPORTANT THING IS, AFTER ALL, TO MEET AND HAVE A GOOD TIME.
AND WEAR A SPECIAL CLUB TIE.

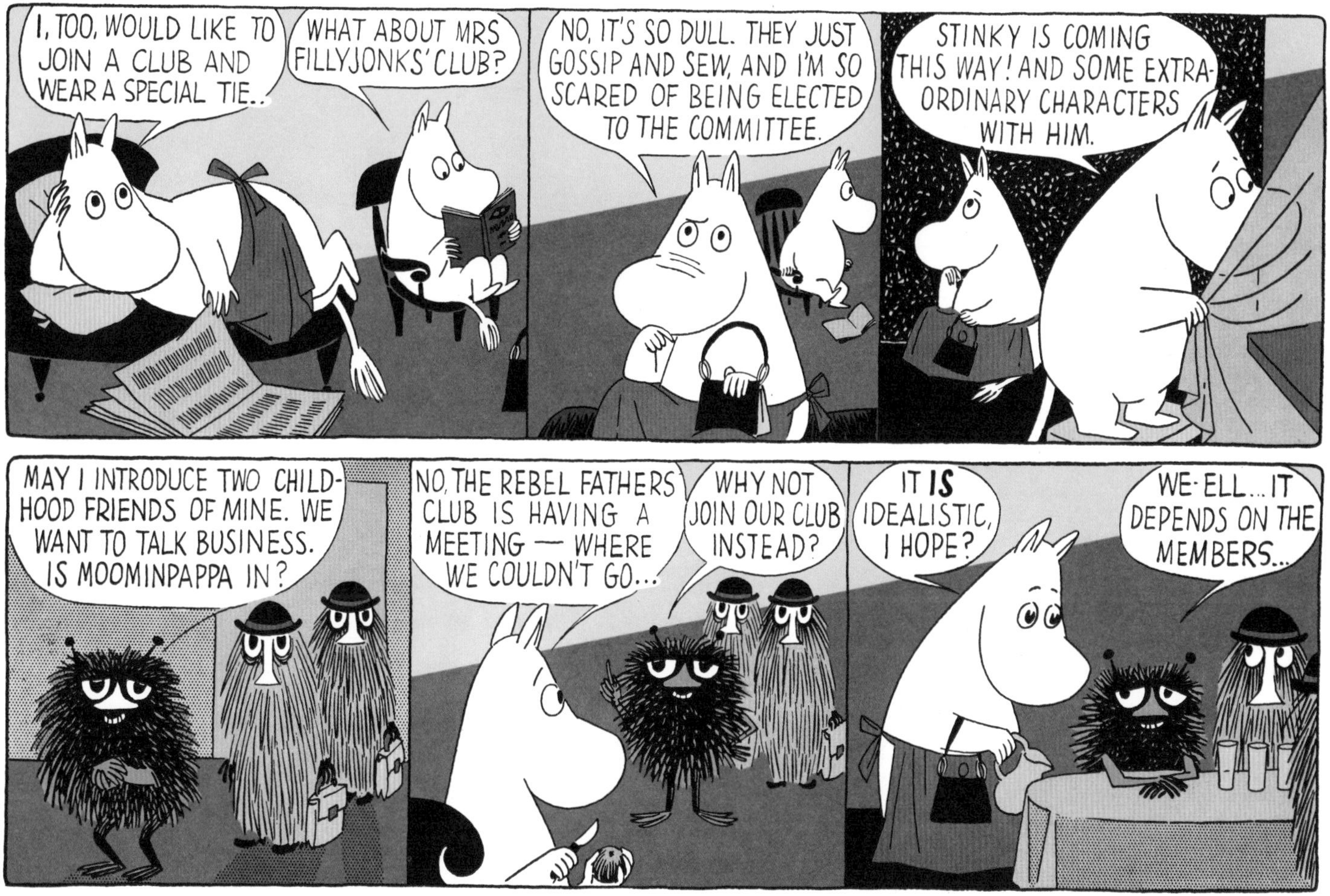
I, TOO, WOULD LIKE TO JOIN A CLUB AND WEAR A SPECIAL TIE..
WHAT ABOUT MRS FILLYJONKS' CLUB?
NO, IT'S SO DULL. THEY JUST GOSSIP AND SEW, AND I'M SO SCARED OF BEING ELECTED TO THE COMMITTEE.
STINKY IS COMING THIS WAY! AND SOME EXTRA-ORDINARY CHARACTERS WITH HIM.
MAY I INTRODUCE TWO CHILD-HOOD FRIENDS OF MINE. WE WANT TO TALK BUSINESS. IS MOOMINPAPPA IN?
NO, THE REBEL FATHERS' CLUB IS HAVING A MEETING — WHERE WE COULDN'T GO...
WHY NOT JOIN OUR CLUB INSTEAD?
IT **IS** IDEALISTIC, I HOPE?
WE-ELL... IT DEPENDS ON THE MEMBERS...

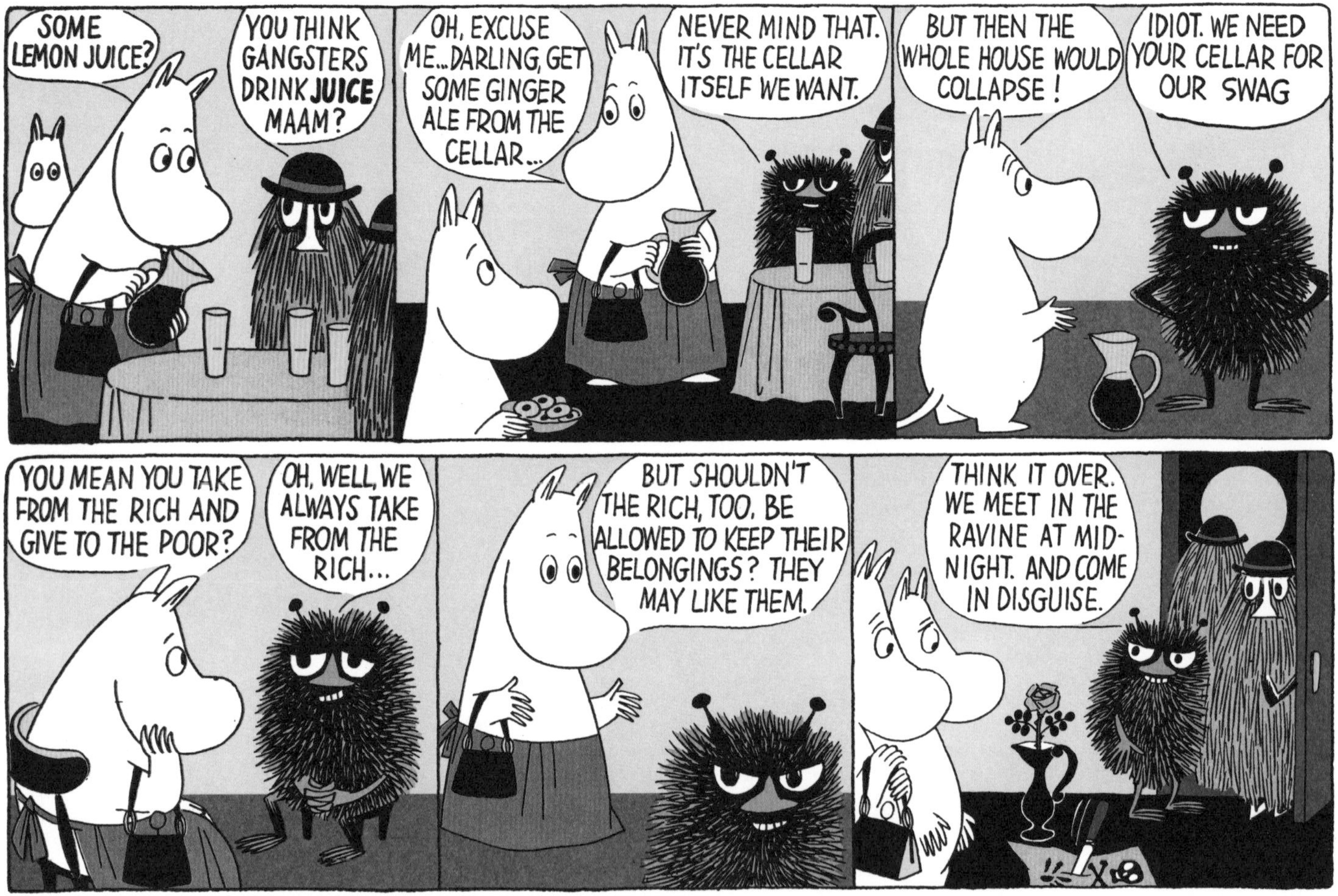
SOME LEMON JUICE?
YOU THINK GANGSTERS DRINK JUICE MAAM?
OH, EXCUSE ME...DARLING, GET SOME GINGER ALE FROM THE CELLAR...
NEVER MIND THAT. IT'S THE CELLAR ITSELF WE WANT.
BUT THEN THE WHOLE HOUSE WOULD COLLAPSE!
IDIOT. WE NEED YOUR CELLAR FOR OUR SWAG
YOU MEAN YOU TAKE FROM THE RICH AND GIVE TO THE POOR?
OH, WELL, WE ALWAYS TAKE FROM THE RICH...
BUT SHOULDN'T THE RICH, TOO, BE ALLOWED TO KEEP THEIR BELONGINGS? THEY MAY LIKE THEM.
THINK IT OVER. WE MEET IN THE RAVINE AT MID-NIGHT. AND COME IN DISGUISE.

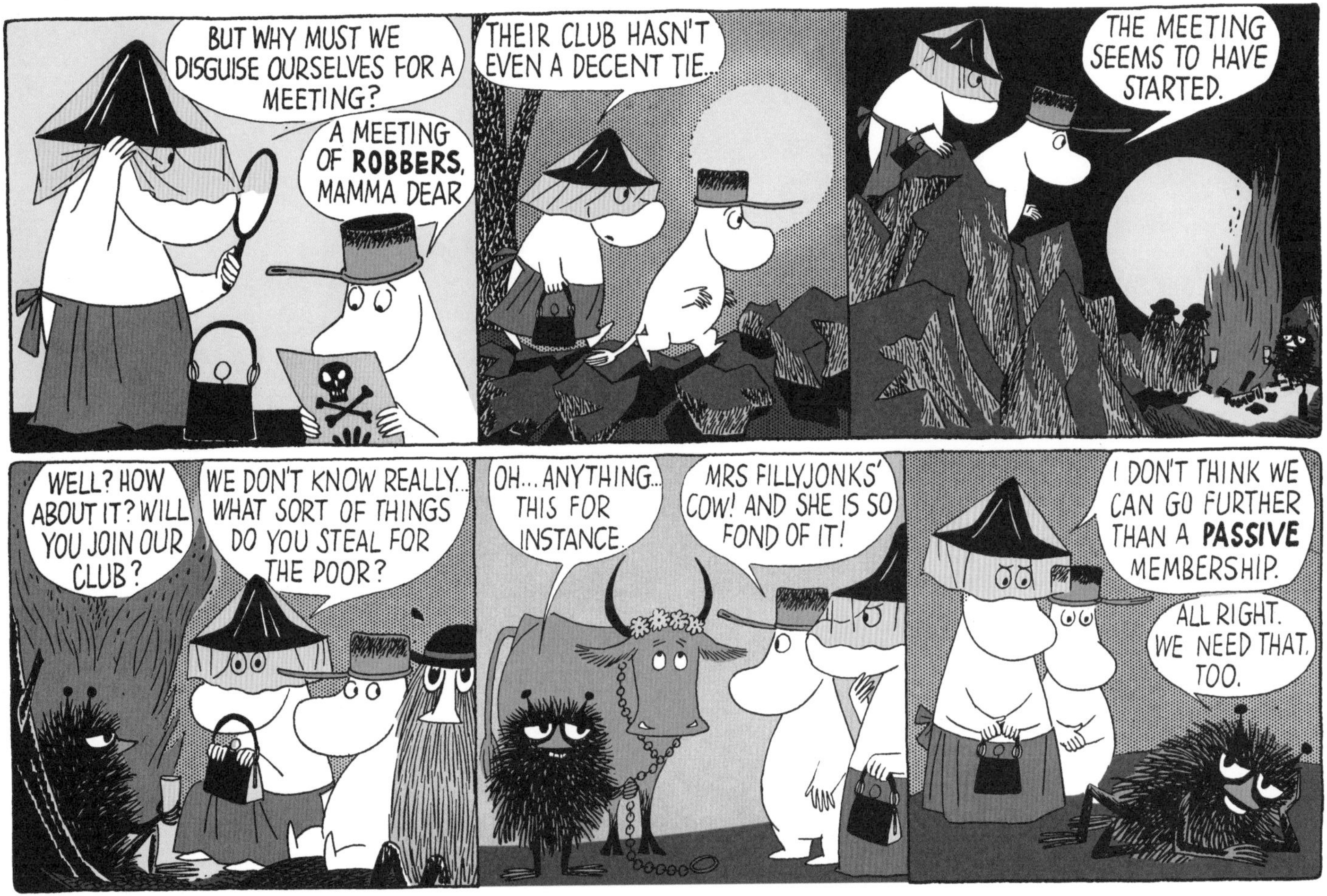
BUT WHY MUST WE DISGUISE OURSELVES FOR A MEETING?
A MEETING OF **ROBBERS**, MAMMA DEAR
THEIR CLUB HASN'T EVEN A DECENT TIE...
THE MEETING SEEMS TO HAVE STARTED.
WELL? HOW ABOUT IT? WILL YOU JOIN OUR CLUB?
WE DON'T KNOW REALLY... WHAT SORT OF THINGS DO YOU STEAL FOR THE POOR?
OH... ANYTHING... THIS FOR INSTANCE.
MRS FILLYJONKS' COW! AND SHE IS SO FOND OF IT!
I DON'T THINK WE CAN GO FURTHER THAN A **PASSIVE** MEMBERSHIP.
ALL RIGHT. WE NEED THAT, TOO.

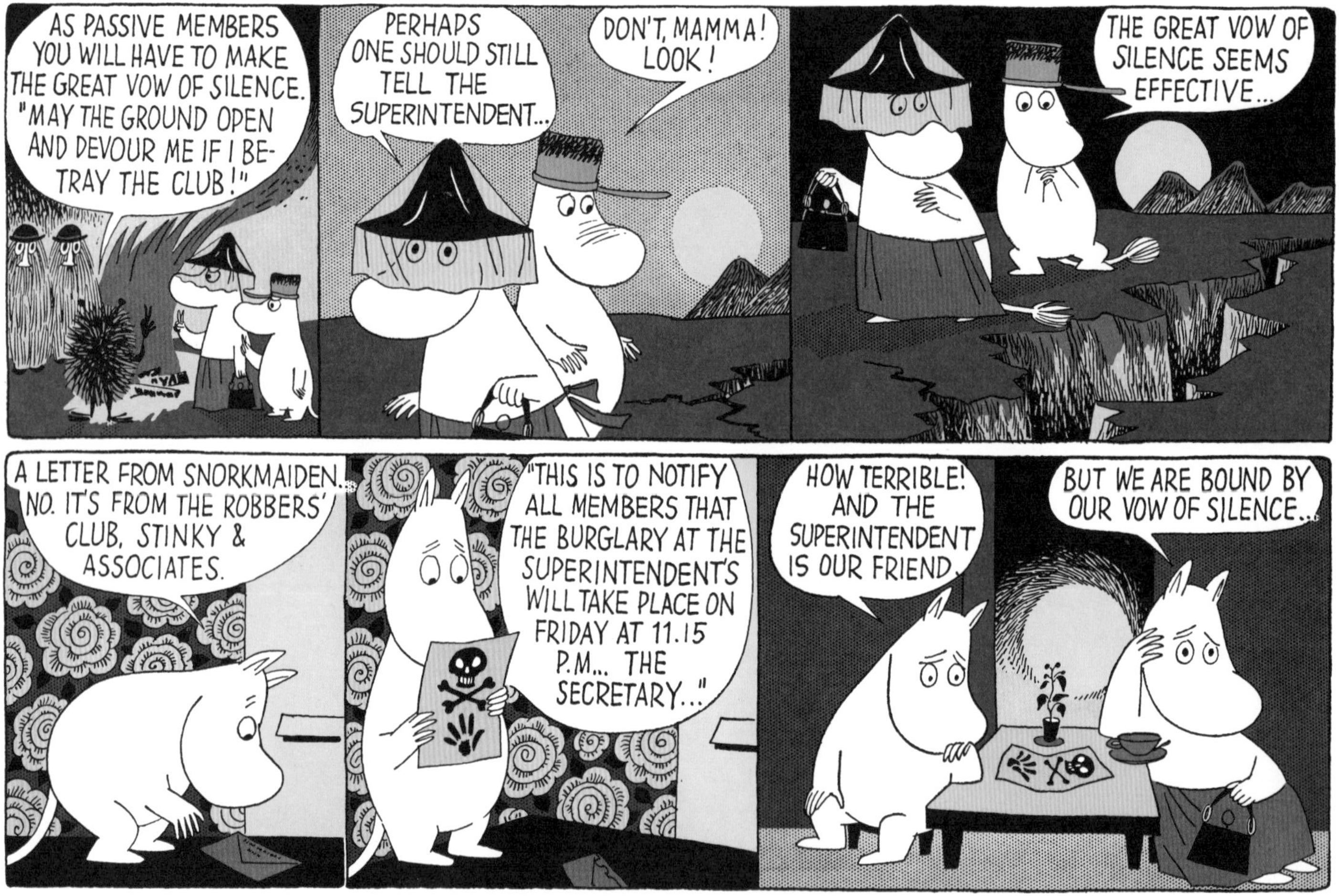
AS PASSIVE MEMBERS YOU WILL HAVE TO MAKE THE GREAT VOW OF SILENCE. "MAY THE GROUND OPEN AND DEVOUR ME IF I BE-TRAY THE CLUB!"
PERHAPS ONE SHOULD STILL TELL THE SUPERINTENDENT...
DON'T, MAMMA! LOOK!
THE GREAT VOW OF SILENCE SEEMS EFFECTIVE...
A LETTER FROM SNORKMAIDEN... NO. IT'S FROM THE ROBBERS' CLUB, STINKY & ASSOCIATES.
"THIS IS TO NOTIFY ALL MEMBERS THAT THE BURGLARY AT THE SUPERINTENDENT'S WILL TAKE PLACE ON FRIDAY AT 11.15 P.M... THE SECRETARY..."
HOW TERRIBLE! AND THE SUPERINTENDENT IS OUR FRIEND.
BUT WE ARE BOUND BY OUR VOW OF SILENCE...

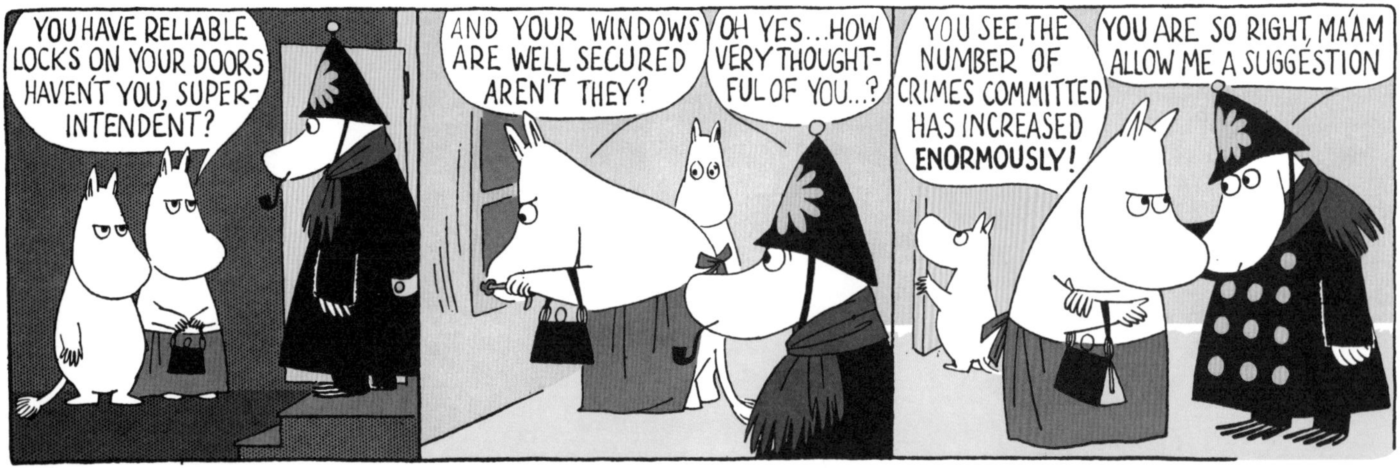
YOU HAVE RELIABLE LOCKS ON YOUR DOORS HAVEN'T YOU, SUPER-INTENDENT?
AND YOUR WINDOWS ARE WELL SECURED AREN'T THEY?
OH YES...HOW VERY THOUGHT-FUL OF YOU...?
YOU SEE, THE NUMBER OF CRIMES COMMITTED HAS INCREASED **ENORMOUSLY**!
YOU ARE SO RIGHT, MA'AM ALLOW ME A SUGGESTION

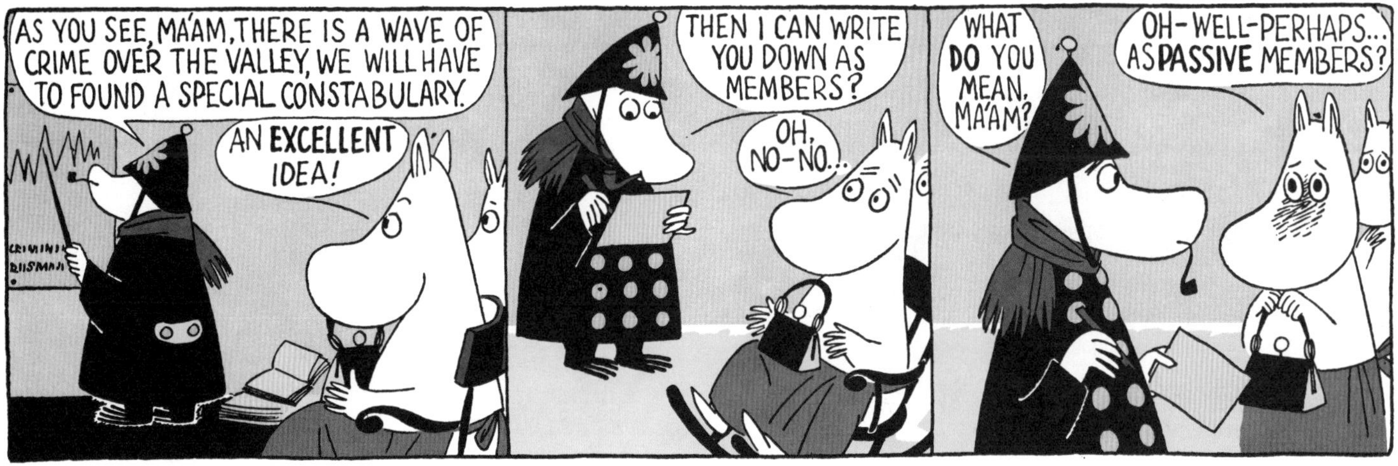
AS YOU SEE, MA'AM, THERE IS A WAVE OF CRIME OVER THE VALLEY, WE WILL HAVE TO FOUND A SPECIAL CONSTABULARY.
AN **EXCELLENT** IDEA!
THEN I CAN WRITE YOU DOWN AS MEMBERS?
OH, NO-NO...
WHAT **DO** YOU MEAN, MA'AM?
OH-WELL-PERHAPS... AS **PASSIVE** MEMBERS?

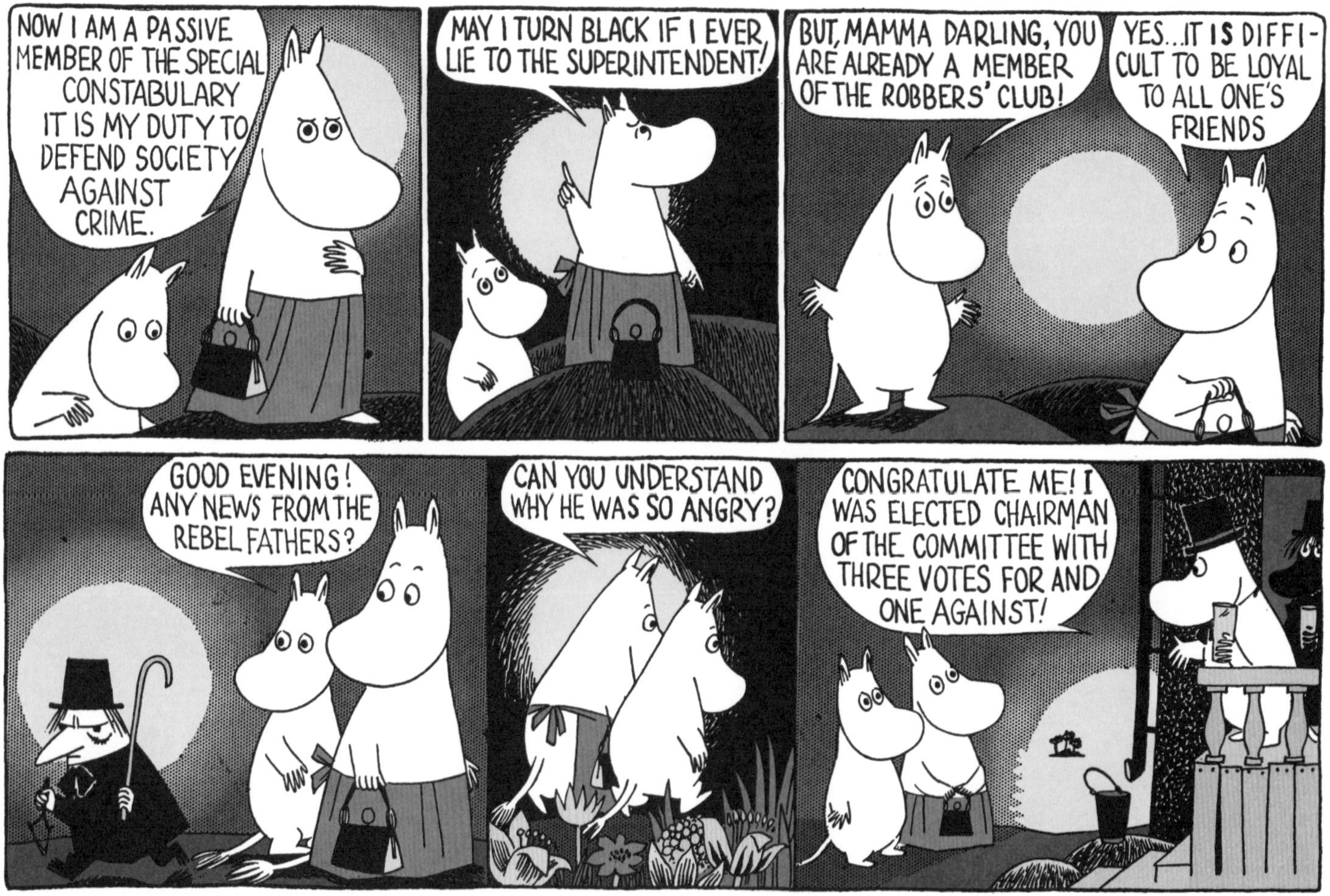
NOW I AM A PASSIVE MEMBER OF THE SPECIAL CONSTABULARY IT IS MY DUTY TO DEFEND SOCIETY AGAINST CRIME.
MAY I TURN BLACK IF I EVER LIE TO THE SUPERINTENDENT!
BUT, MAMMA DARLING, YOU ARE ALREADY A MEMBER OF THE ROBBERS' CLUB!
YES...IT **IS** DIFFICULT TO BE LOYAL TO ALL ONE'S FRIENDS
GOOD EVENING! ANY NEWS FROM THE REBEL FATHERS?
CAN YOU UNDERSTAND WHY HE WAS SO ANGRY?
CONGRATULATE ME! I WAS ELECTED CHAIRMAN OF THE COMMITTEE WITH THREE VOTES FOR AND ONE AGAINST!

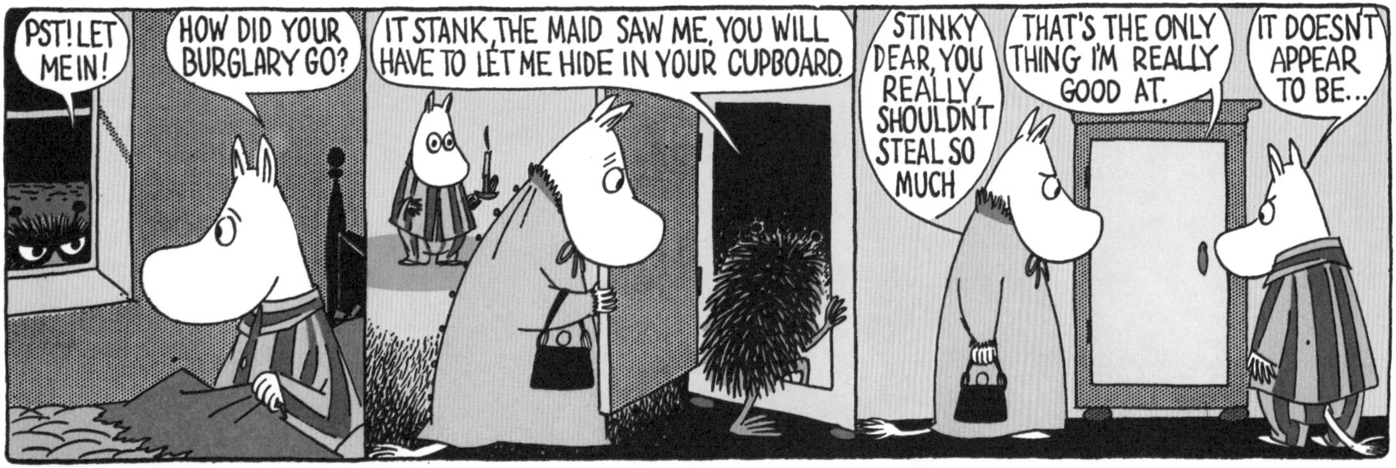
PST! LET ME IN!
HOW DID YOUR BURGLARY GO?
IT STANK, THE MAID SAW ME, YOU WILL HAVE TO LET ME HIDE IN YOUR CUPBOARD.
STINKY DEAR, YOU REALLY SHOULDN'T STEAL SO MUCH
THAT'S THE ONLY THING I'M REALLY GOOD AT.
IT DOESN'T APPEAR TO BE...

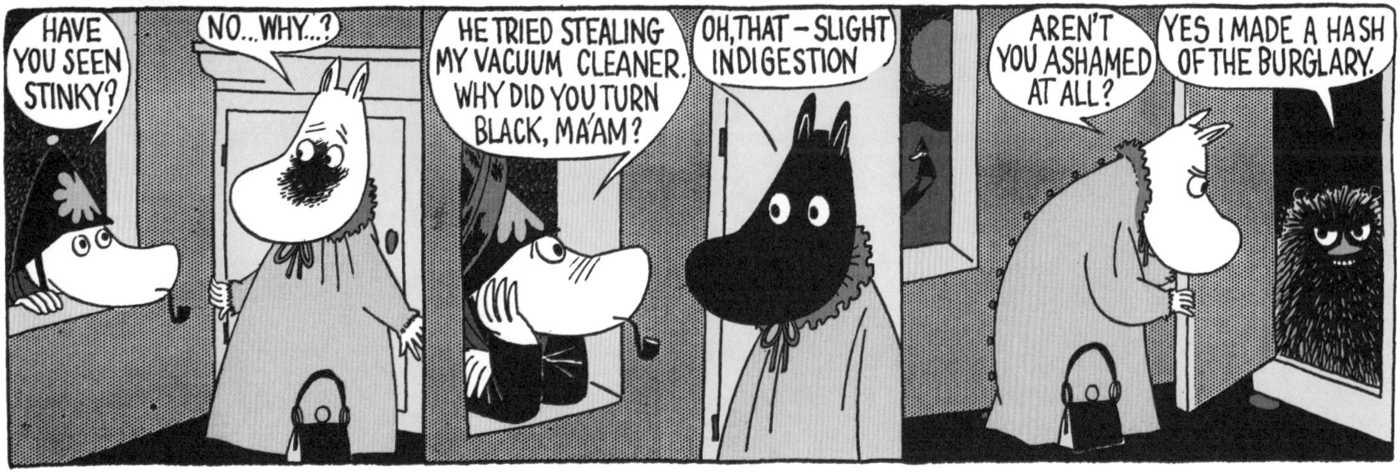
HAVE YOU SEEN STINKY?
NO... WHY..?
HE TRIED STEALING MY VACUUM CLEANER. WHY DID YOU TURN BLACK, MA'AM?
OH, THAT – SLIGHT INDIGESTION
AREN'T YOU ASHAMED AT ALL?
YES I MADE A HASH OF THE BURGLARY.

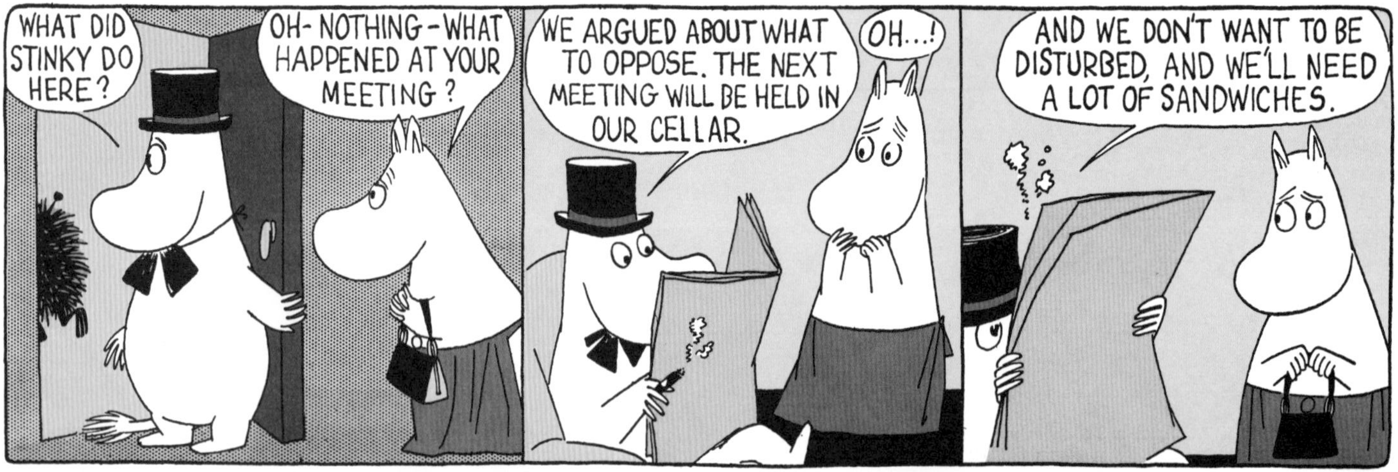
WHAT DID STINKY DO HERE?
OH- NOTHING - WHAT HAPPENED AT YOUR MEETING?
WE ARGUED ABOUT WHAT TO OPPOSE. THE NEXT MEETING WILL BE HELD IN OUR CELLAR.
OH...!
AND WE DON'T WANT TO BE DISTURBED, AND WE'LL NEED A LOT OF SANDWICHES.

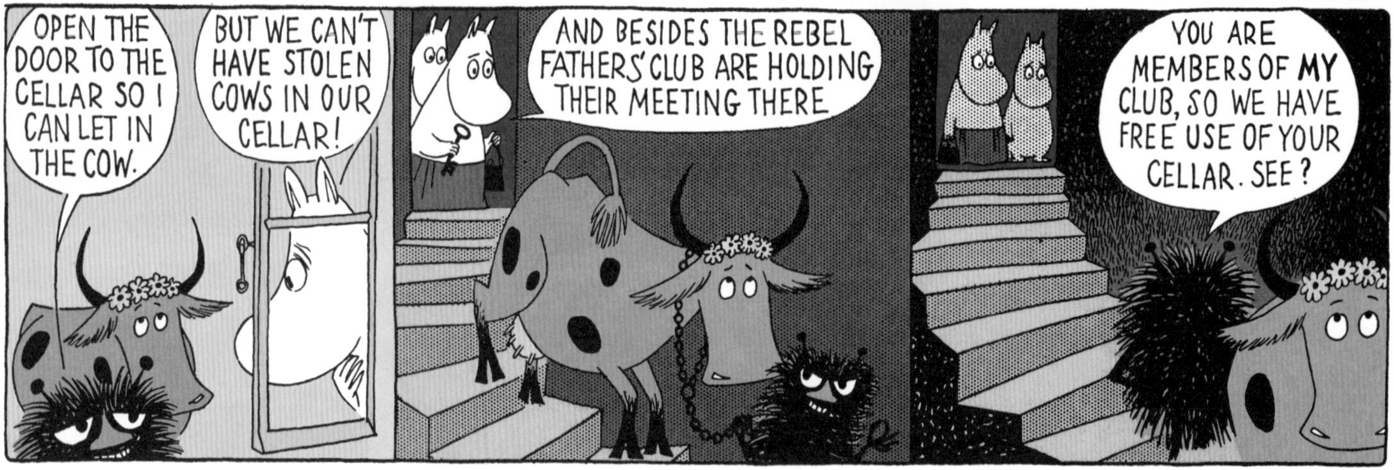
OPEN THE DOOR TO THE CELLAR SO I CAN LET IN THE COW.
BUT WE CAN'T HAVE STOLEN COWS IN OUR CELLAR!
AND BESIDES THE REBEL FATHERS' CLUB ARE HOLDING THEIR MEETING THERE
YOU ARE MEMBERS OF **MY** CLUB, SO WE HAVE FREE USE OF YOUR CELLAR. SEE?

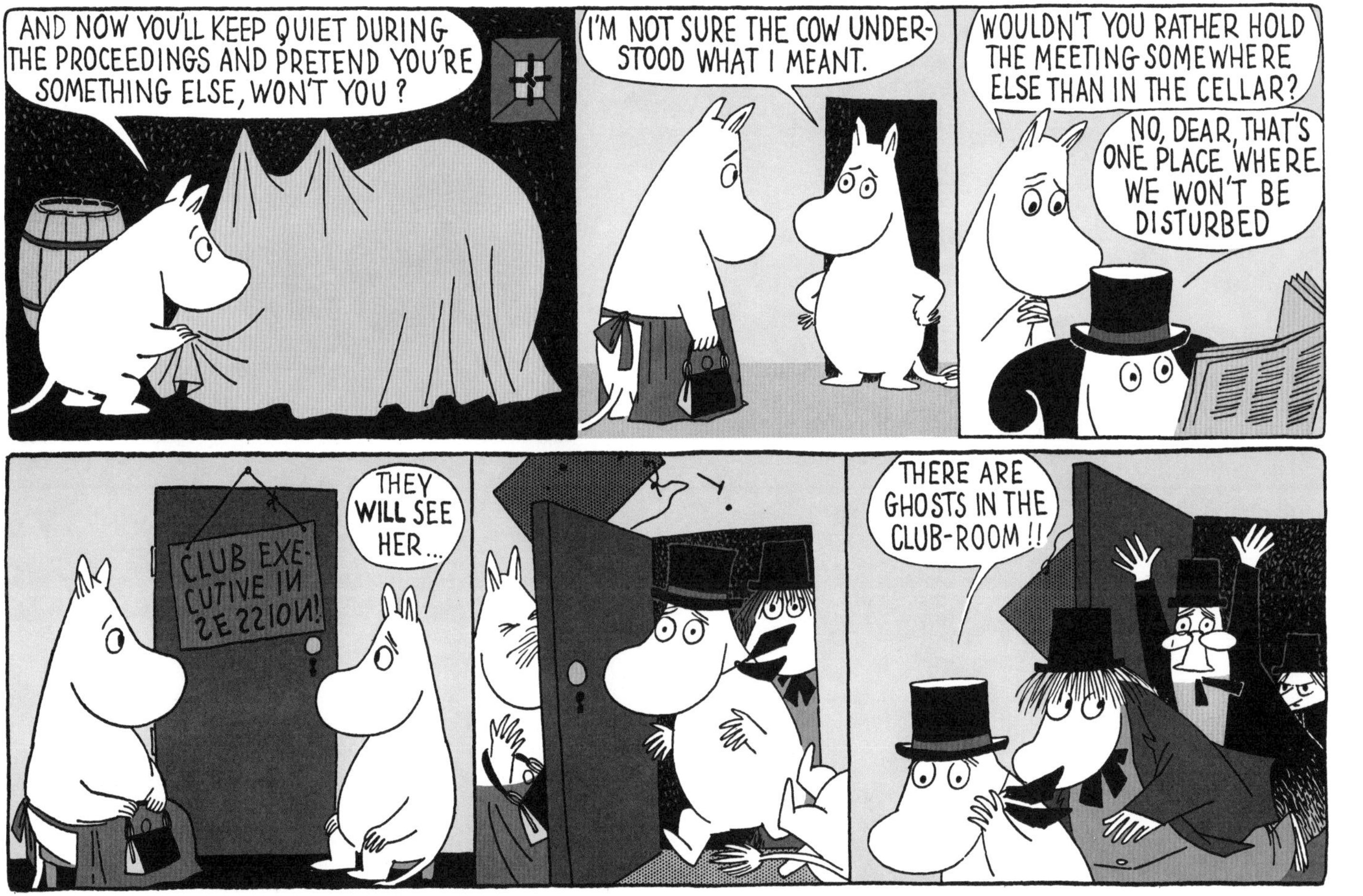

AND NOW YOU'LL KEEP QUIET DURING THE PROCEEDINGS AND PRETEND YOU'RE SOMETHING ELSE, WON'T YOU ?
I'M NOT SURE THE COW UNDERSTOOD WHAT I MEANT.
WOULDN'T YOU RATHER HOLD THE MEETING SOMEWHERE ELSE THAN IN THE CELLAR?
NO, DEAR, THAT'S ONE PLACE WHERE WE WON'T BE DISTURBED
CLUB EXECUTIVE IN SESSION!
THEY **WILL** SEE HER...
THERE ARE GHOSTS IN THE CLUB-ROOM !!

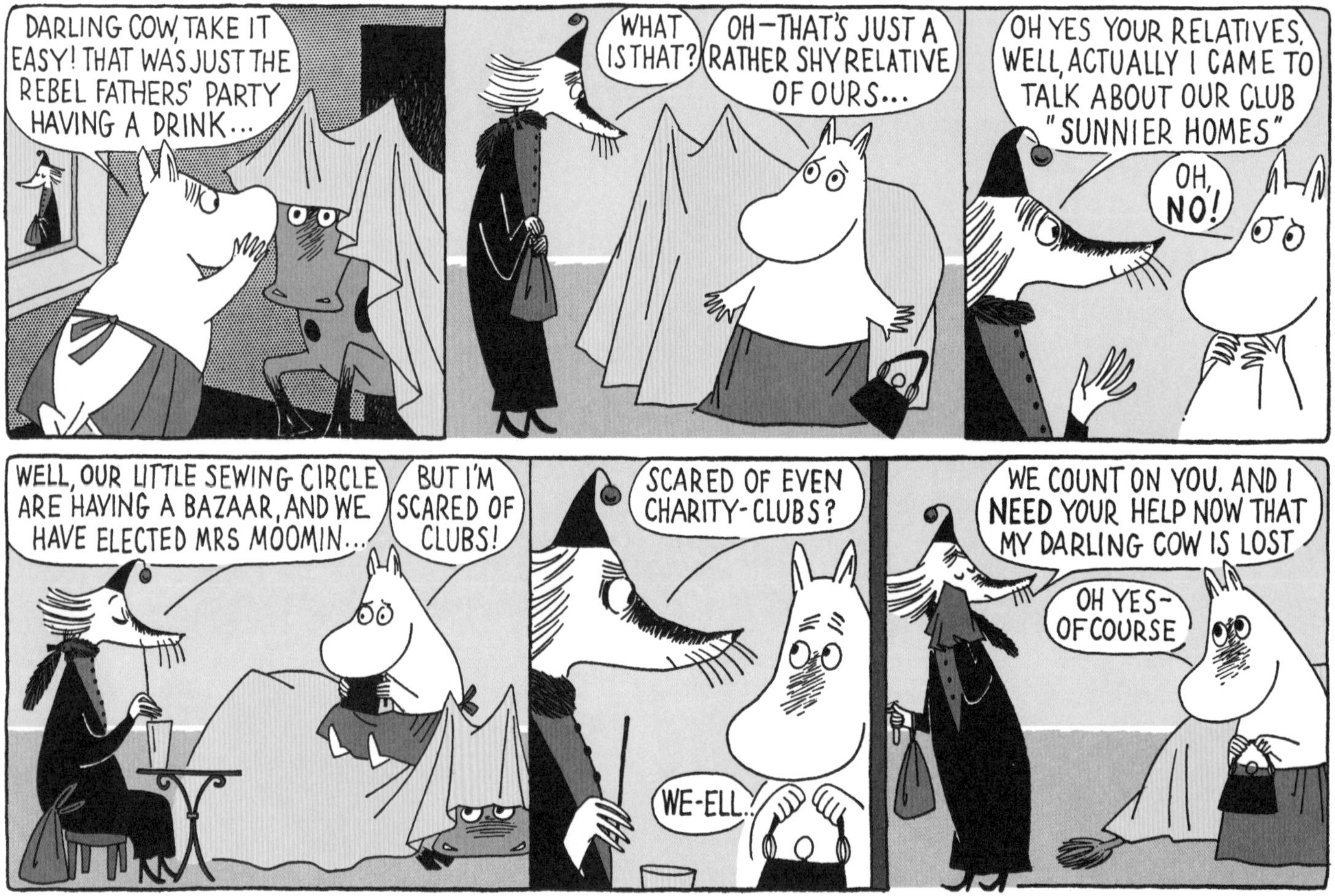
DARLING COW, TAKE IT EASY! THAT WAS JUST THE REBEL FATHERS' PARTY HAVING A DRINK...
WHAT IS THAT?
OH—THAT'S JUST A RATHER SHY RELATIVE OF OURS...
OH YES YOUR RELATIVES. WELL, ACTUALLY I CAME TO TALK ABOUT OUR CLUB "SUNNIER HOMES"
OH, NO!
WELL, OUR LITTLE SEWING CIRCLE ARE HAVING A BAZAAR, AND WE HAVE ELECTED MRS MOOMIN...
BUT I'M SCARED OF CLUBS!
SCARED OF EVEN CHARITY-CLUBS?
WE-ELL..
WE COUNT ON YOU. AND I NEED YOUR HELP NOW THAT MY DARLING COW IS LOST
OH YES-OF COURSE

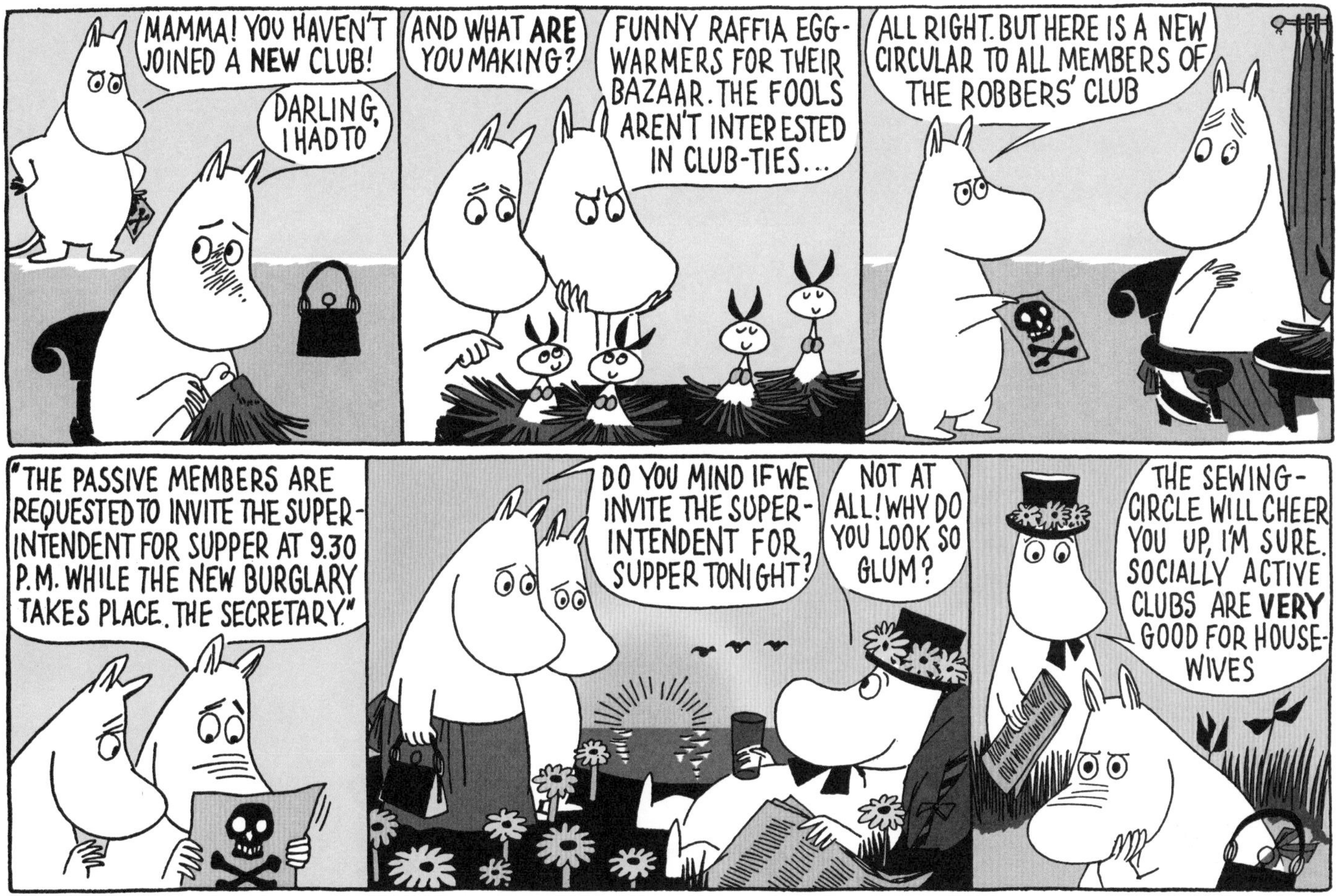
MAMMA! YOU HAVEN'T JOINED A NEW CLUB!
DARLING, I HAD TO
AND WHAT ARE YOU MAKING?
FUNNY RAFFIA EGG-WARMERS FOR THEIR BAZAAR. THE FOOLS AREN'T INTERESTED IN CLUB-TIES...
ALL RIGHT. BUT HERE IS A NEW CIRCULAR TO ALL MEMBERS OF THE ROBBERS' CLUB
"THE PASSIVE MEMBERS ARE REQUESTED TO INVITE THE SUPER-INTENDENT FOR SUPPER AT 9.30 P.M. WHILE THE NEW BURGLARY TAKES PLACE. THE SECRETARY."
DO YOU MIND IF WE INVITE THE SUPER-INTENDENT FOR SUPPER TONIGHT?
NOT AT ALL! WHY DO YOU LOOK SO GLUM?
THE SEWING-CIRCLE WILL CHEER YOU UP, I'M SURE. SOCIALLY ACTIVE CLUBS ARE VERY GOOD FOR HOUSE-WIVES

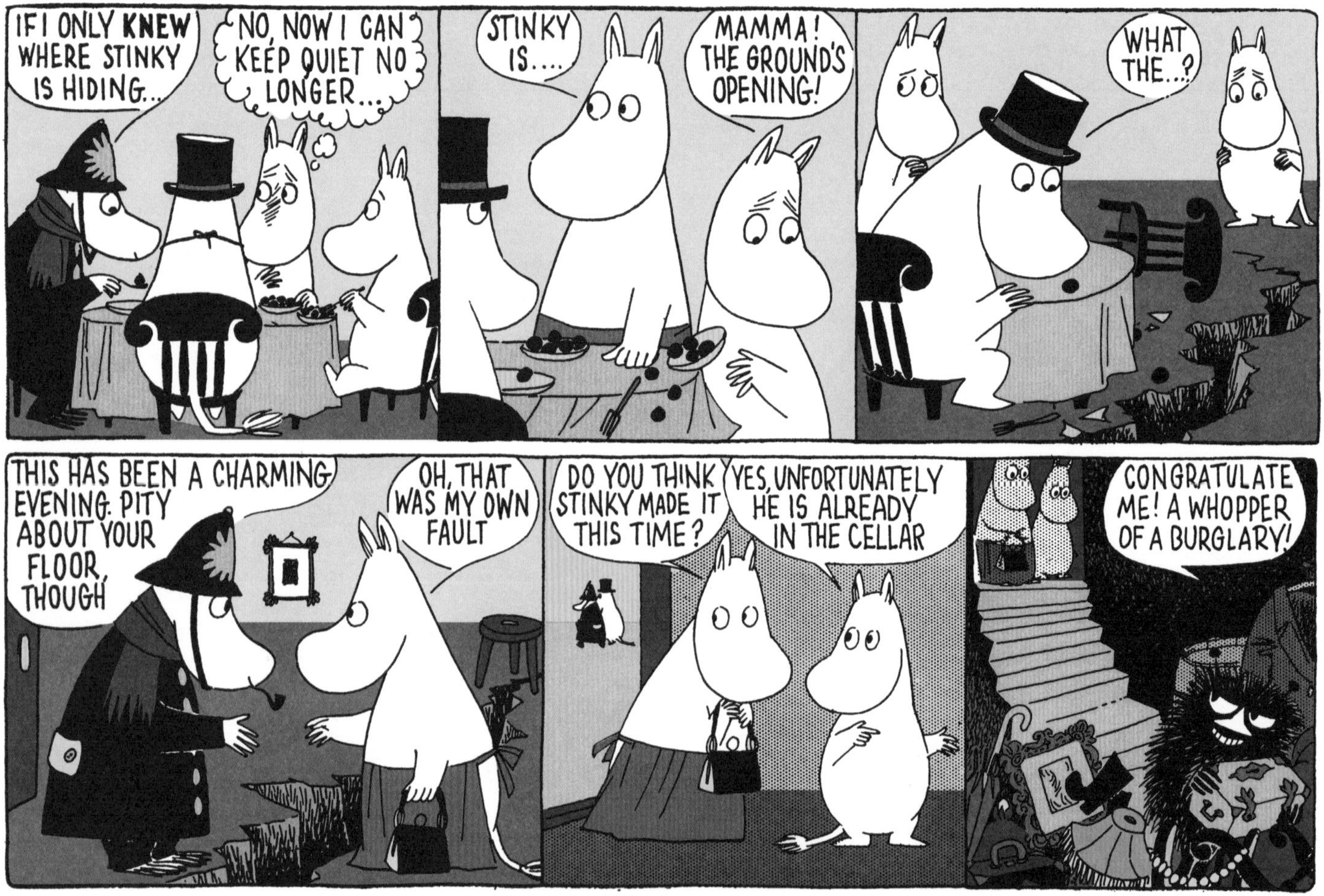
IF I ONLY KNEW WHERE STINKY IS HIDING...
NO, NOW I CAN KEEP QUIET NO LONGER...
STINKY IS....
MAMMA! THE GROUND'S OPENING!
WHAT THE...?
THIS HAS BEEN A CHARMING EVENING. PITY ABOUT YOUR FLOOR, THOUGH
OH, THAT WAS MY OWN FAULT
DO YOU THINK STINKY MADE IT THIS TIME?
YES, UNFORTUNATELY HE IS ALREADY IN THE CELLAR
CONGRATULATE ME! A WHOPPER OF A BURGLARY!

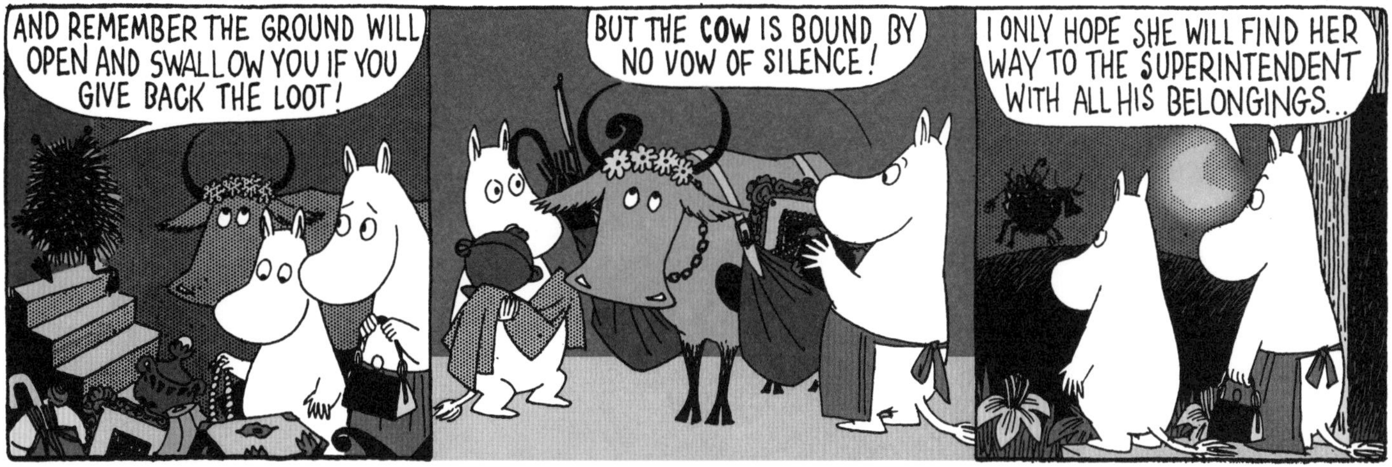
AND REMEMBER THE GROUND WILL OPEN AND SWALLOW YOU IF YOU GIVE BACK THE LOOT!
BUT THE COW IS BOUND BY NO VOW OF SILENCE!
I ONLY HOPE SHE WILL FIND HER WAY TO THE SUPERINTENDENT WITH ALL HIS BELONGINGS...

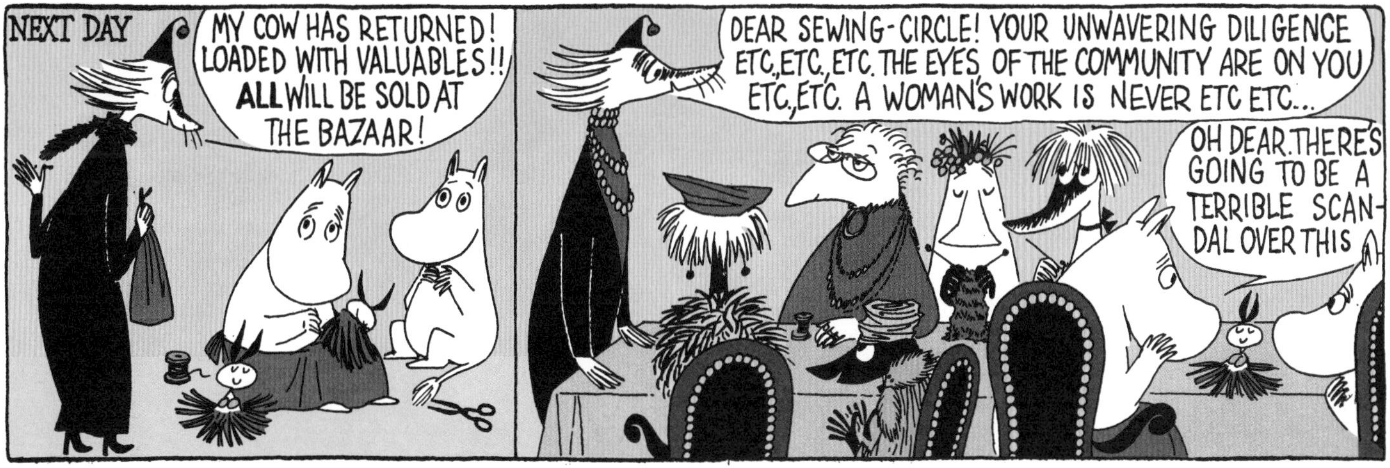
NEXT DAY
MY COW HAS RETURNED! LOADED WITH VALUABLES!! ALL WILL BE SOLD AT THE BAZAAR!
DEAR SEWING-CIRCLE! YOUR UNWAVERING DILIGENCE ETC.,ETC.,ETC. THE EYES OF THE COMMUNITY ARE ON YOU ETC.,ETC. A WOMAN'S WORK IS NEVER ETC ETC...
OH DEAR. THERE'S GOING TO BE A TERRIBLE SCANDAL OVER THIS

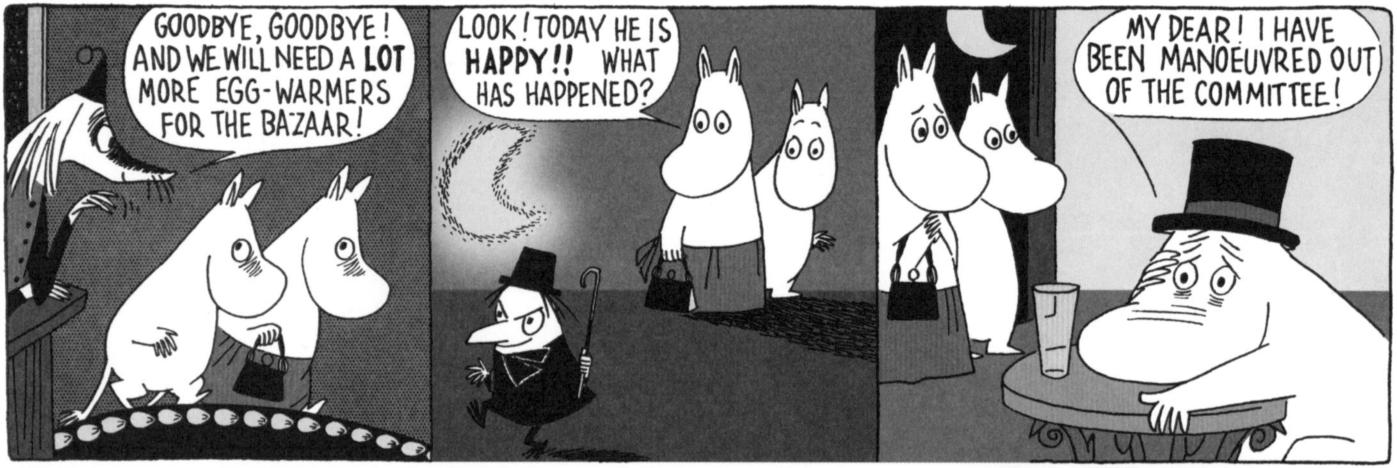
GOODBYE, GOODBYE! AND WE WILL NEED A **LOT** MORE EGG-WARMERS FOR THE BAZAAR!
LOOK! TODAY HE IS **HAPPY!!** WHAT HAS HAPPENED?
MY DEAR! I HAVE BEEN MANOEUVRED OUT OF THE COMMITTEE!

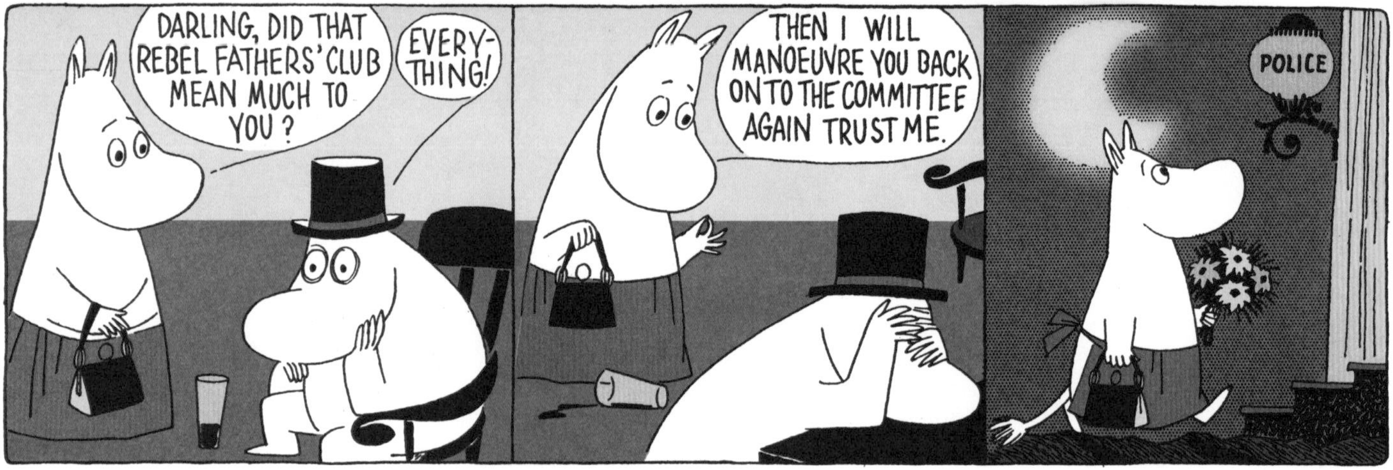
DARLING, DID THAT REBEL FATHERS' CLUB MEAN MUCH TO YOU?
EVERY-THING!
THEN I WILL MANOEUVRE YOU BACK ON TO THE COMMITTEE AGAIN TRUST ME.
POLICE

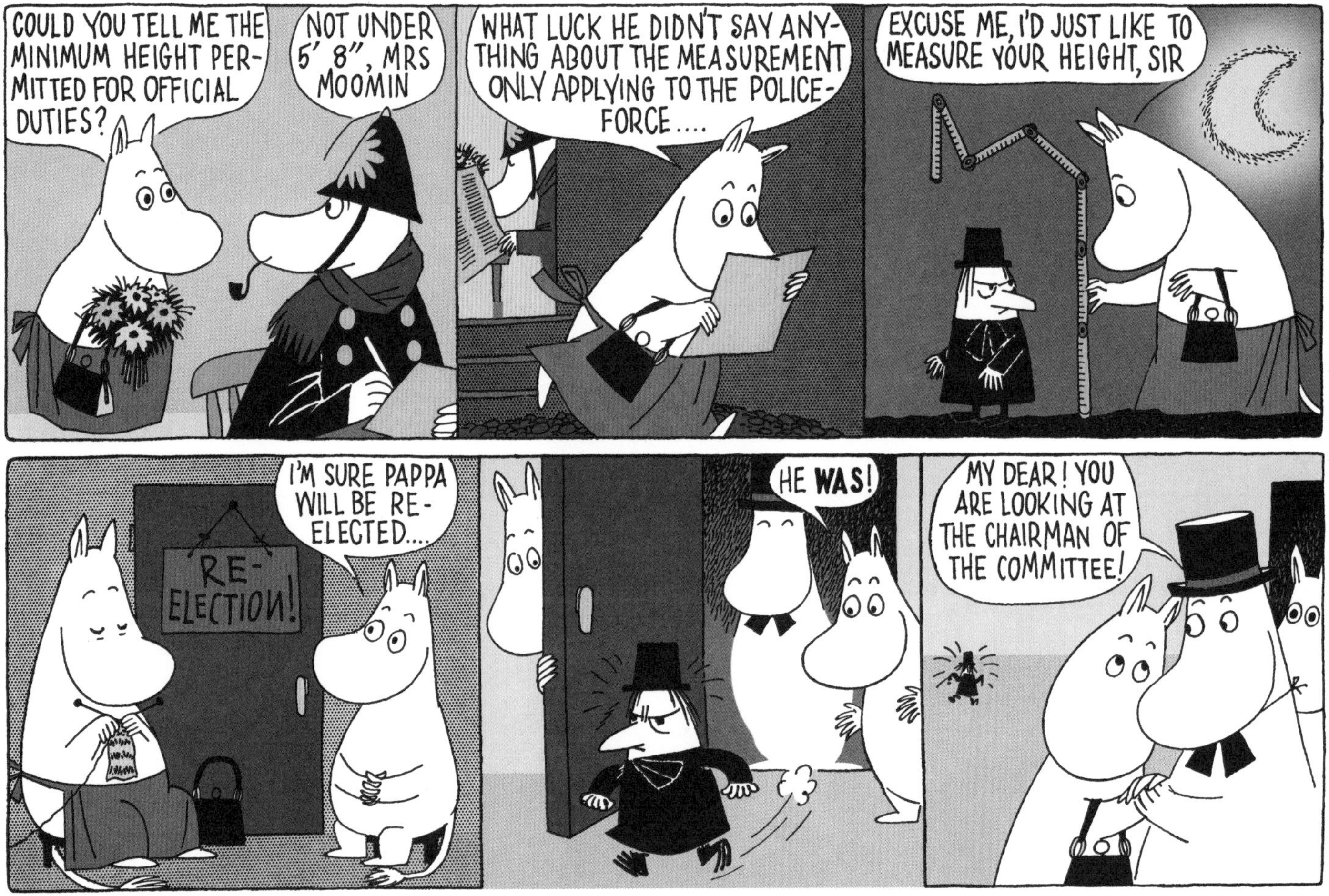
COULD YOU TELL ME THE MINIMUM HEIGHT PERMITTED FOR OFFICIAL DUTIES?
NOT UNDER 5' 8", MRS MOOMIN
WHAT LUCK HE DIDN'T SAY ANYTHING ABOUT THE MEASUREMENT ONLY APPLYING TO THE POLICE-FORCE....
EXCUSE ME, I'D JUST LIKE TO MEASURE YOUR HEIGHT, SIR
RE-ELECTION!
I'M SURE PAPPA WILL BE RE-ELECTED....
HE WAS!
MY DEAR! YOU ARE LOOKING AT THE CHAIRMAN OF THE COMMITTEE!

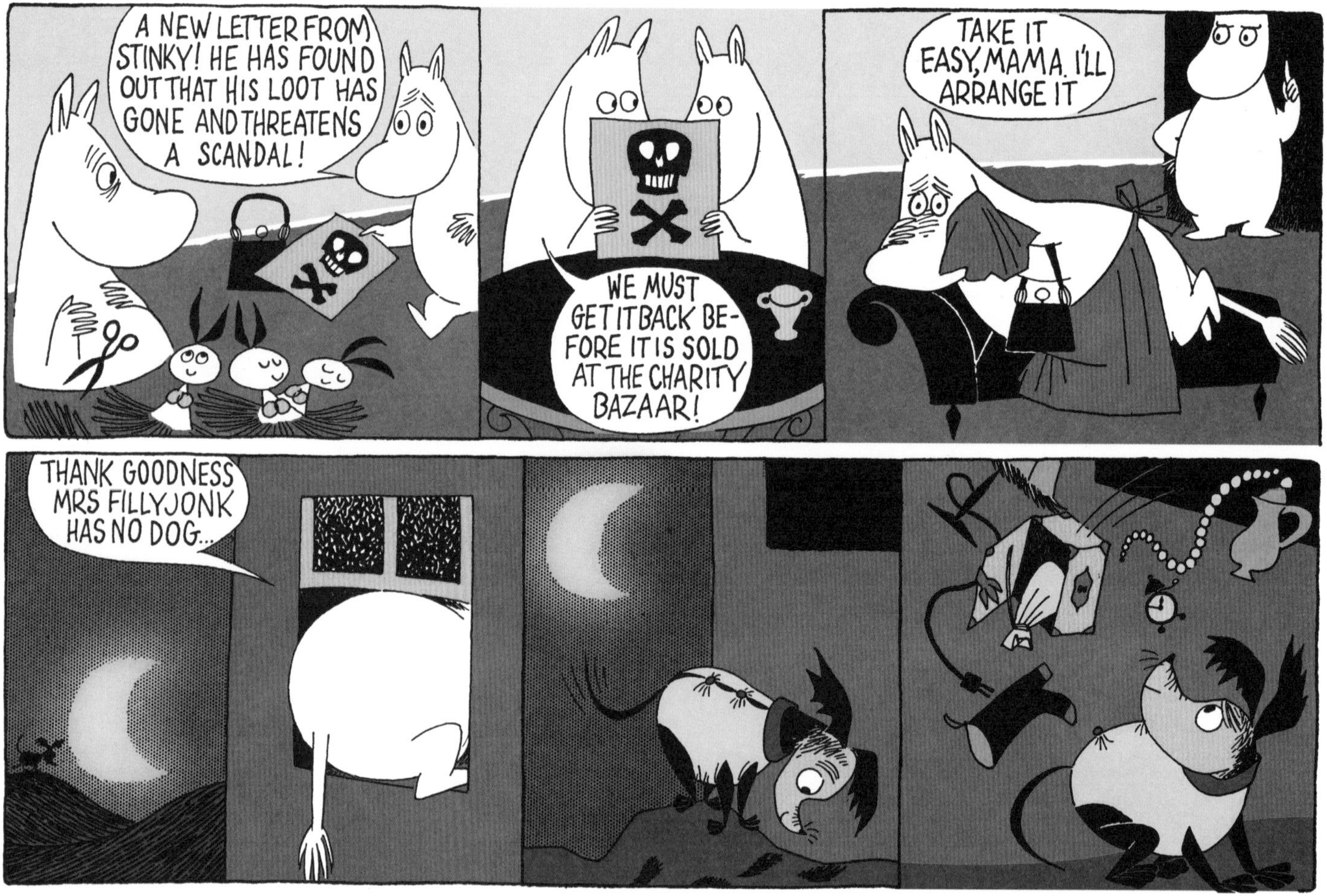

A NEW LETTER FROM STINKY! HE HAS FOUND OUT THAT HIS LOOT HAS GONE AND THREATENS A SCANDAL!
WE MUST GET IT BACK BE-FORE IT IS SOLD AT THE CHARITY BAZAAR!
TAKE IT EASY, MAMA. I'LL ARRANGE IT
THANK GOODNESS MRS FILLYJONK HAS NO DOG...

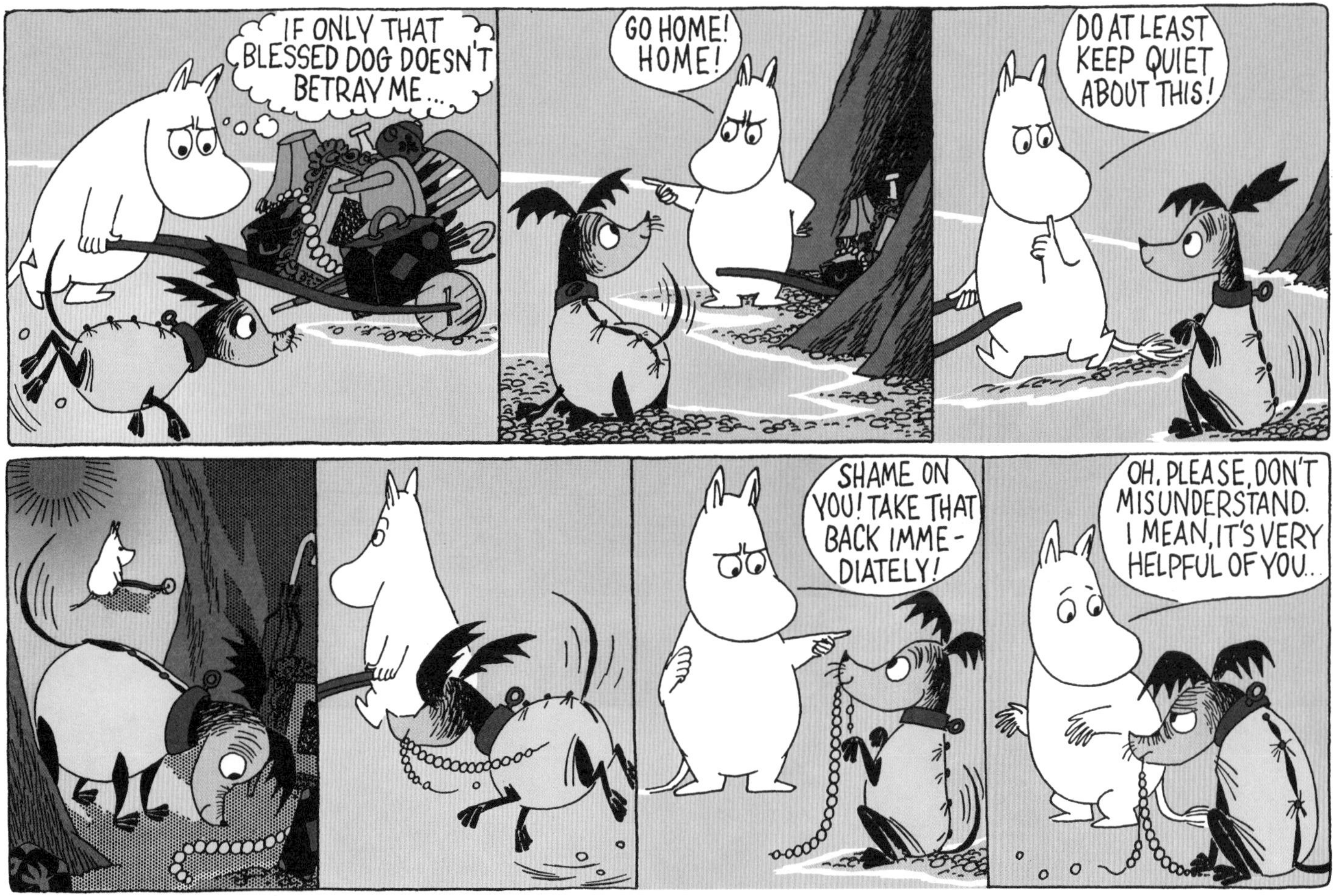
IF ONLY THAT BLESSED DOG DOESN'T BETRAY ME...
GO HOME! HOME!
DO AT LEAST KEEP QUIET ABOUT THIS!
SHAME ON YOU! TAKE THAT BACK IMME-DIATELY!
OH, PLEASE, DON'T MISUNDERSTAND. I MEAN, IT'S VERY HELPFUL OF YOU..

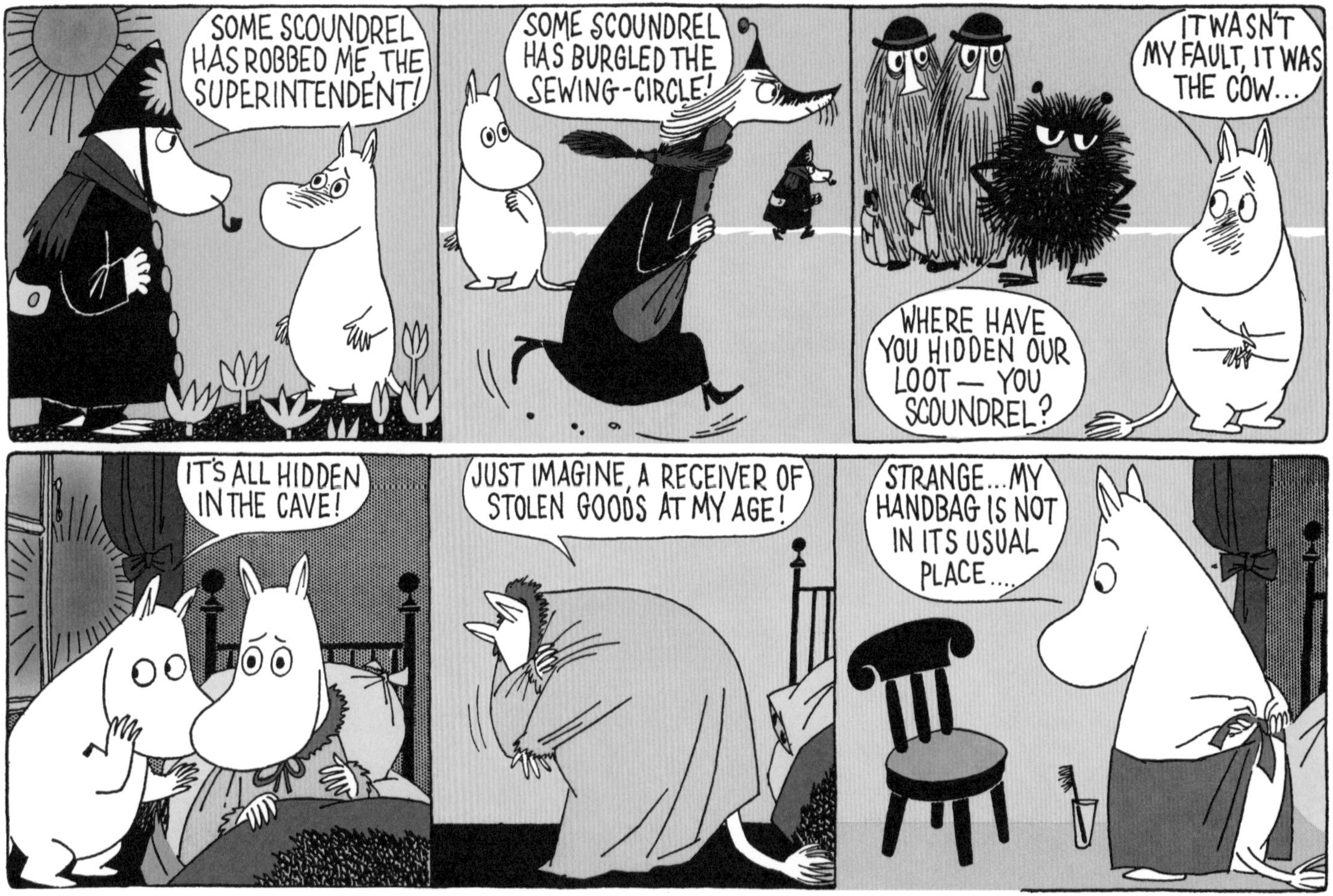
SOME SCOUNDREL HAS ROBBED ME, THE SUPERINTENDENT!
SOME SCOUNDREL HAS BURGLED THE SEWING-CIRCLE!
IT WASN'T MY FAULT, IT WAS THE COW...
WHERE HAVE YOU HIDDEN OUR LOOT — YOU SCOUNDREL?
IT'S ALL HIDDEN IN THE CAVE!
JUST IMAGINE, A RECEIVER OF STOLEN GOODS AT MY AGE!
STRANGE...MY HANDBAG IS NOT IN ITS USUAL PLACE....

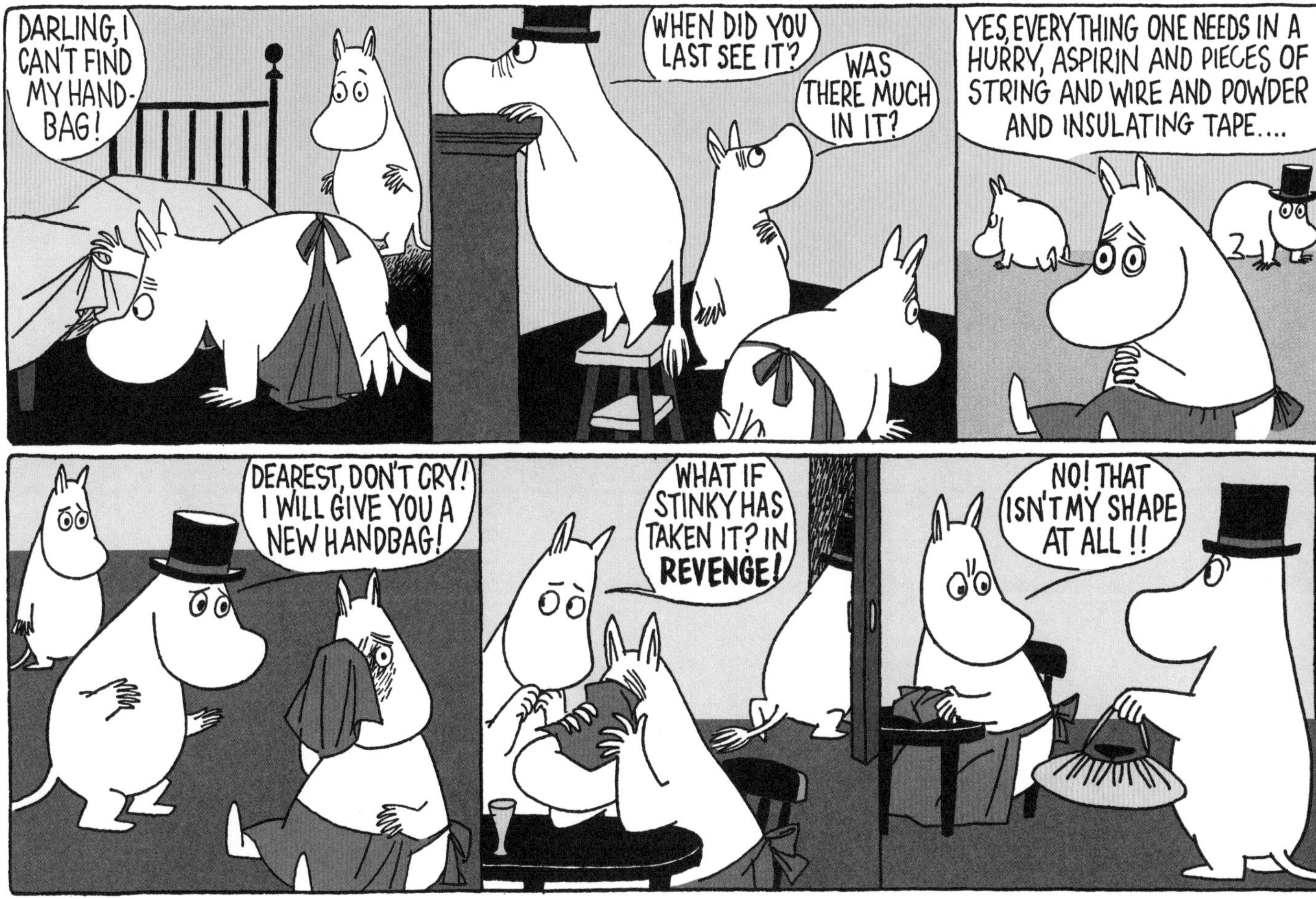
DARLING, I CAN'T FIND MY HAND-BAG!
WHEN DID YOU LAST SEE IT?
WAS THERE MUCH IN IT?
YES, EVERYTHING ONE NEEDS IN A HURRY, ASPIRIN AND PIECES OF STRING AND WIRE AND POWDER AND INSULATING TAPE....
DEAREST, DON'T CRY! I WILL GIVE YOU A NEW HANDBAG!
WHAT IF STINKY HAS TAKEN IT? IN REVENGE!
NO! THAT ISN'T MY SHAPE AT ALL!!

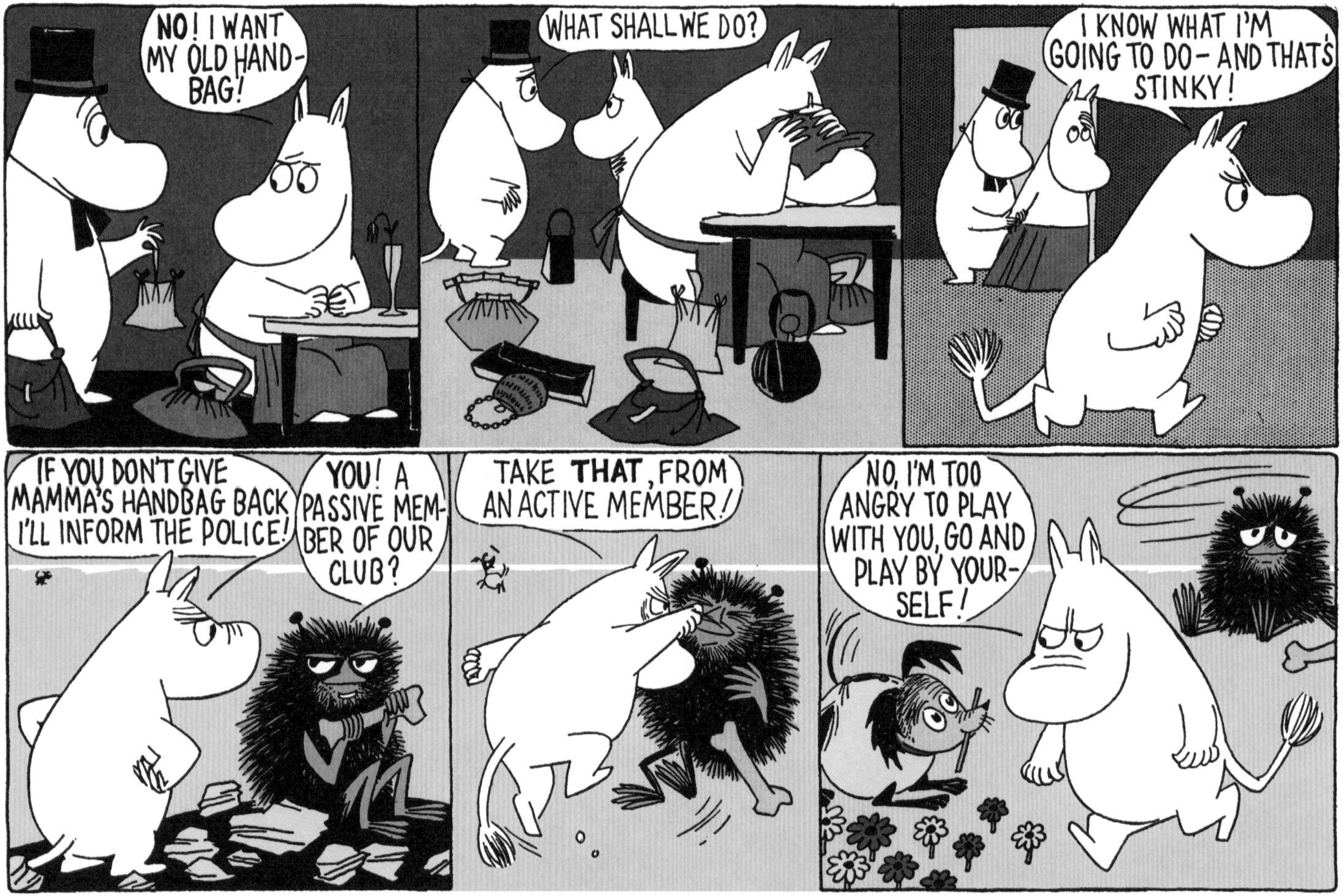
NO! I WANT MY OLD HAND-BAG!
WHAT SHALL WE DO?
I KNOW WHAT I'M GOING TO DO - AND THAT'S STINKY!
IF YOU DON'T GIVE MAMMA'S HANDBAG BACK I'LL INFORM THE POLICE!
YOU! A PASSIVE MEM-BER OF OUR CLUB?
TAKE THAT, FROM AN ACTIVE MEMBER!
NO, I'M TOO ANGRY TO PLAY WITH YOU, GO AND PLAY BY YOUR-SELF!

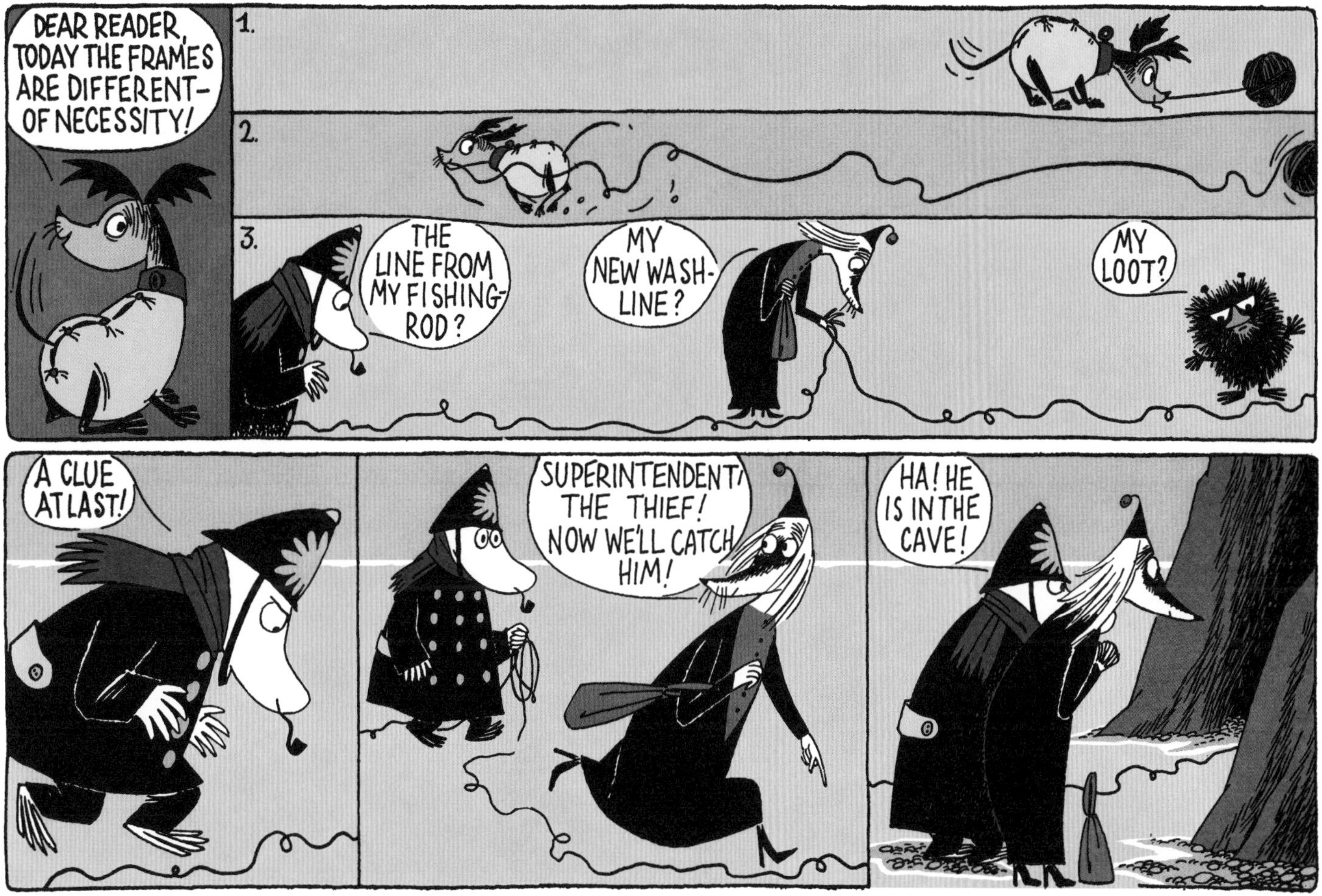
DEAR READER, TODAY THE FRAMES ARE DIFFERENT-OF NECESSITY!
1.
2.
3.
THE LINE FROM MY FISHING-ROD?
MY NEW WASH-LINE?
MY LOOT?
A CLUE AT LAST!
SUPERINTENDENT! THE THIEF! NOW WE'LL CATCH HIM!
HA! HE IS IN THE CAVE!

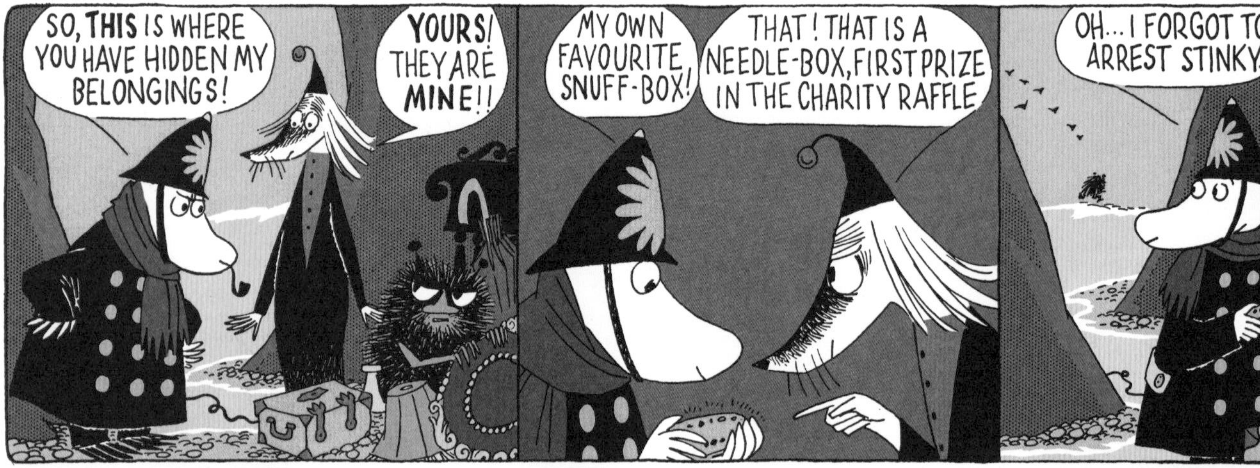
SO, THIS IS WHERE YOU HAVE HIDDEN MY BELONGINGS!
YOURS! THEY ARE MINE!!
MY OWN FAVOURITE SNUFF-BOX!
THAT! THAT IS A NEEDLE-BOX, FIRST PRIZE IN THE CHARITY RAFFLE
OH... I FORGOT TO ARREST STINKY..

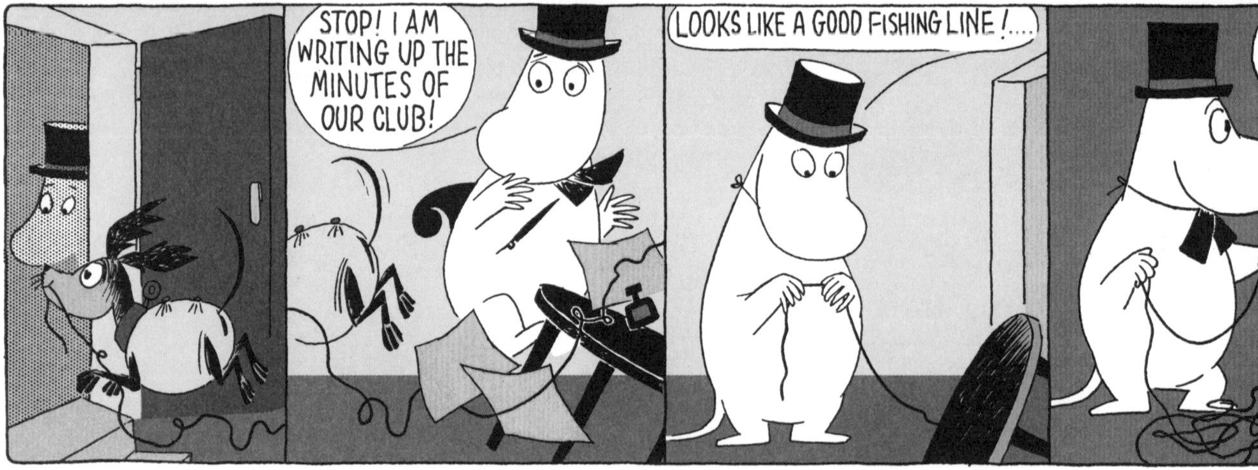
STOP! I AM WRITING UP THE MINUTES OF OUR CLUB!
LOOKS LIKE A GOOD FISHING LINE!....
LET'S SEE HOW LONG IT IS....

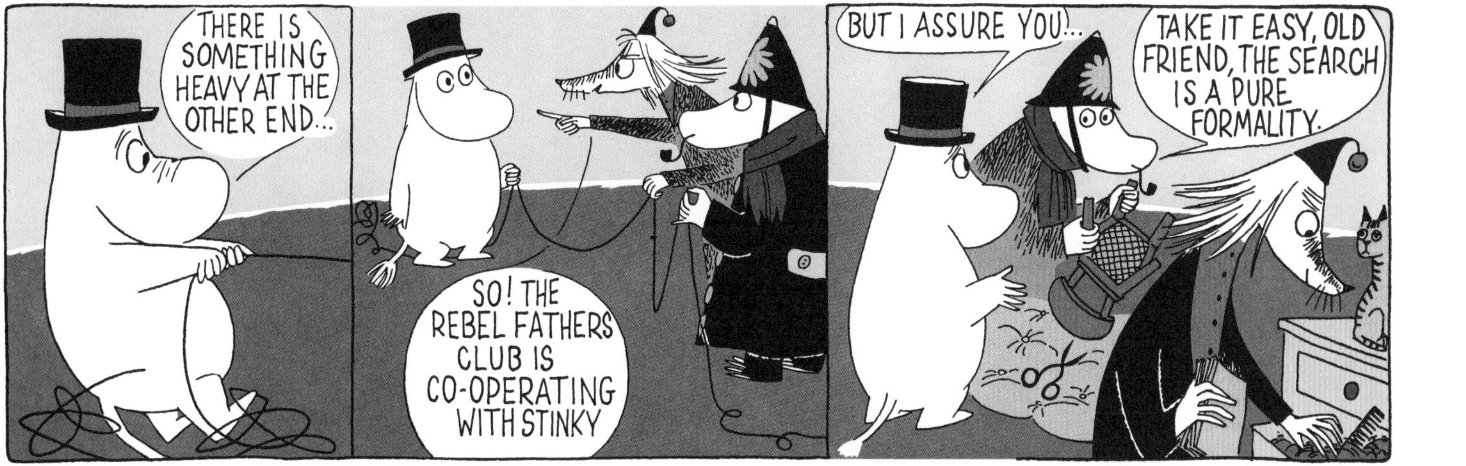
THERE IS SOMETHING HEAVY AT THE OTHER END...
SO! THE REBEL FATHERS CLUB IS CO-OPERATING WITH STINKY
BUT I ASSURE YOU...
TAKE IT EASY, OLD FRIEND, THE SEARCH IS A PURE FORMALITY.

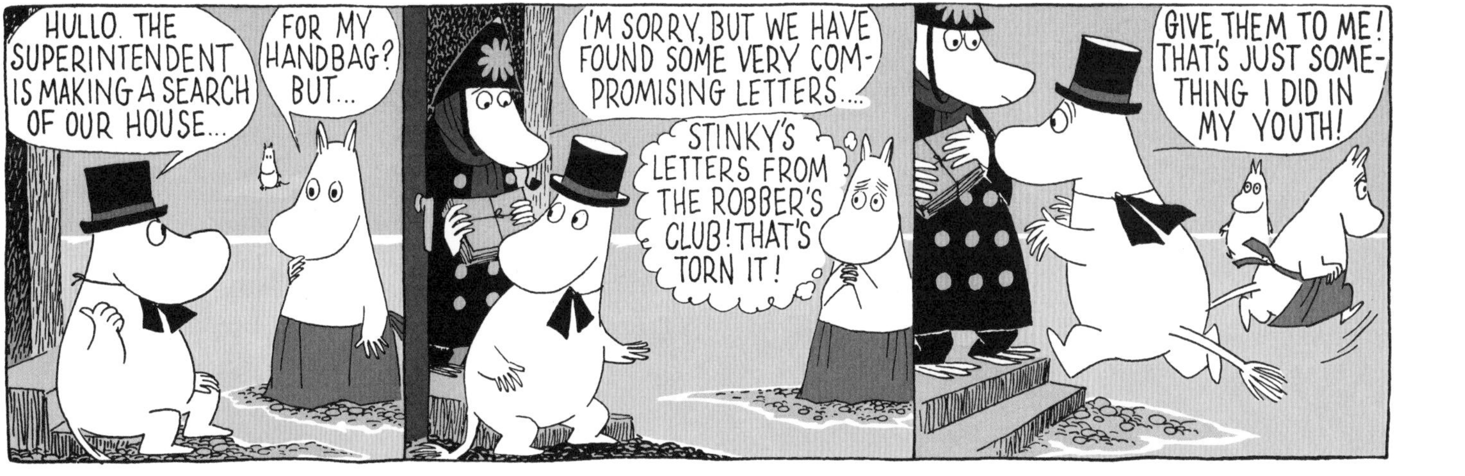
HULLO. THE SUPERINTENDENT IS MAKING A SEARCH OF OUR HOUSE...
FOR MY HANDBAG? BUT...
I'M SORRY, BUT WE HAVE FOUND SOME VERY COM-PROMISING LETTERS....
STINKY'S LETTERS FROM THE ROBBER'S CLUB! THAT'S TORN IT!
GIVE THEM TO ME! THAT'S JUST SOME-THING I DID IN MY YOUTH!

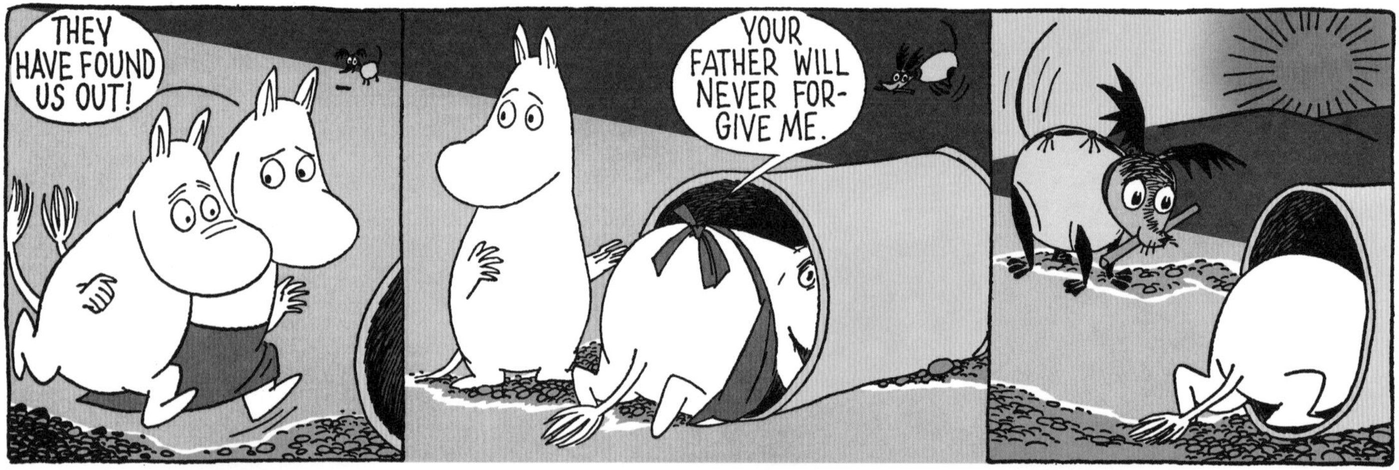
THEY HAVE FOUND US OUT!
YOUR FATHER WILL NEVER FOR-GIVE ME.

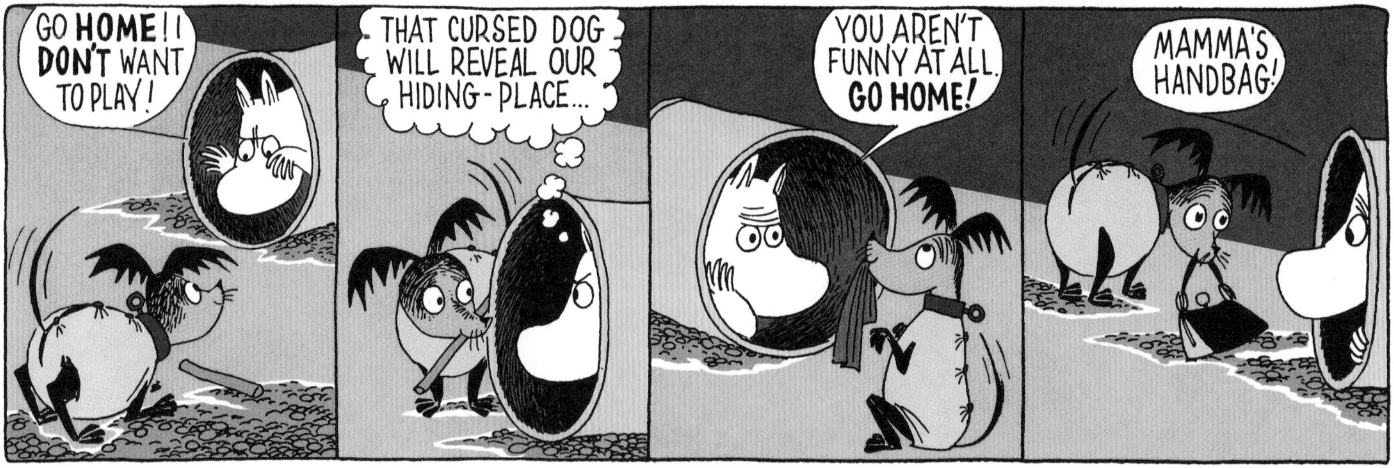
GO HOME!! I DON'T WANT TO PLAY!
THAT CURSED DOG WILL REVEAL OUR HIDING-PLACE...
YOU AREN'T FUNNY AT ALL. GO HOME!
MAMMA'S HANDBAG!

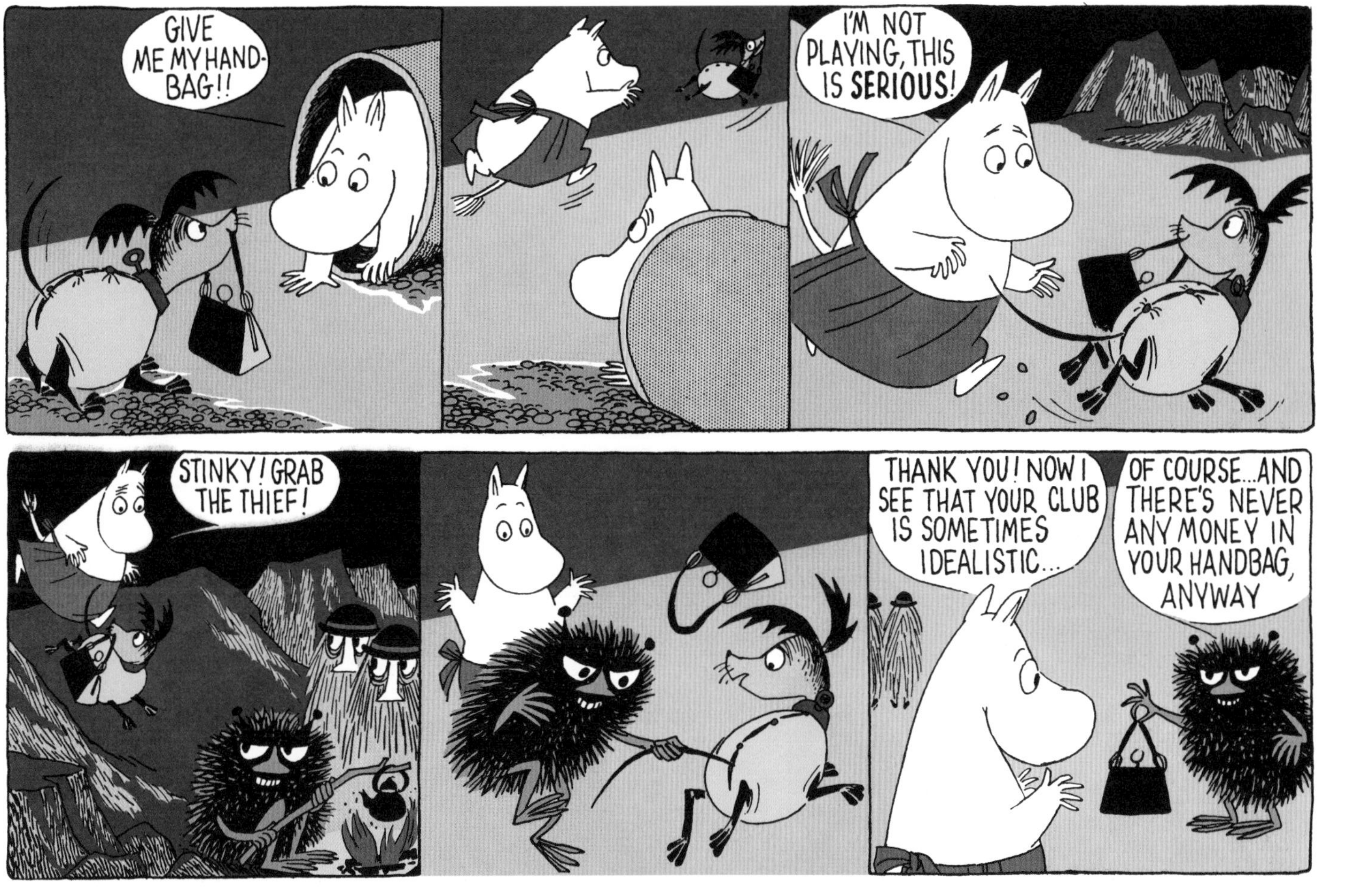
GIVE ME MY HAND-BAG!!
I'M NOT PLAYING, THIS IS **SERIOUS**!
STINKY! GRAB THE THIEF!
THANK YOU! NOW I SEE THAT YOUR CLUB IS SOMETIMES IDEALISTIC...
OF COURSE...AND THERE'S NEVER ANY MONEY IN YOUR HANDBAG, ANYWAY

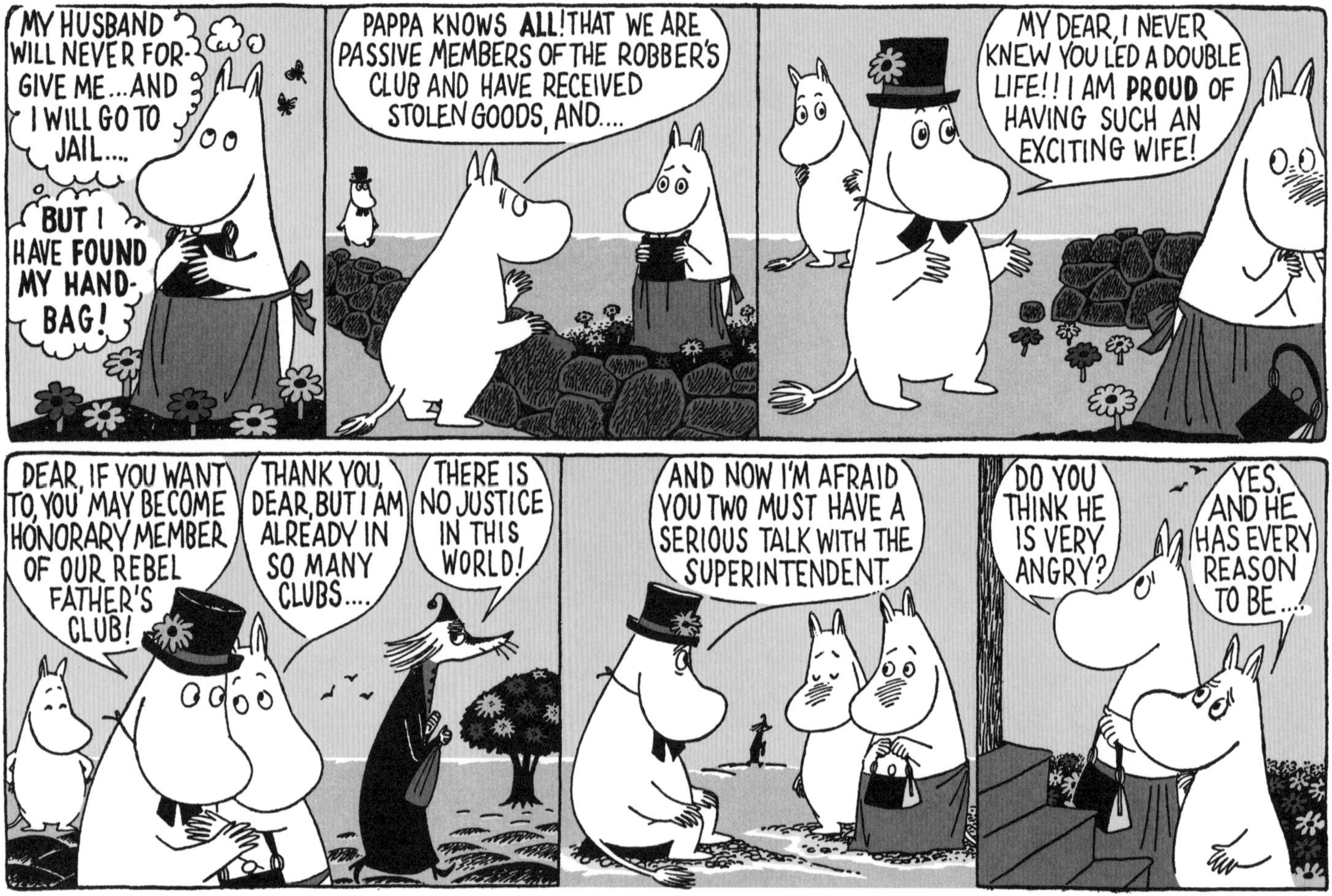
MY HUSBAND WILL NEVER FORGIVE ME...AND I WILL GO TO JAIL....
BUT I HAVE FOUND MY HANDBAG!
PAPPA KNOWS ALL! THAT WE ARE PASSIVE MEMBERS OF THE ROBBER'S CLUB AND HAVE RECEIVED STOLEN GOODS, AND....
MY DEAR, I NEVER KNEW YOU LED A DOUBLE LIFE!! I AM PROUD OF HAVING SUCH AN EXCITING WIFE!
DEAR, IF YOU WANT TO, YOU MAY BECOME HONORARY MEMBER OF OUR REBEL FATHER'S CLUB!
THANK YOU, DEAR, BUT I AM ALREADY IN SO MANY CLUBS....
THERE IS NO JUSTICE IN THIS WORLD!
AND NOW I'M AFRAID YOU TWO MUST HAVE A SERIOUS TALK WITH THE SUPERINTENDENT.
DO YOU THINK HE IS VERY ANGRY?
YES. AND HE HAS EVERY REASON TO BE....

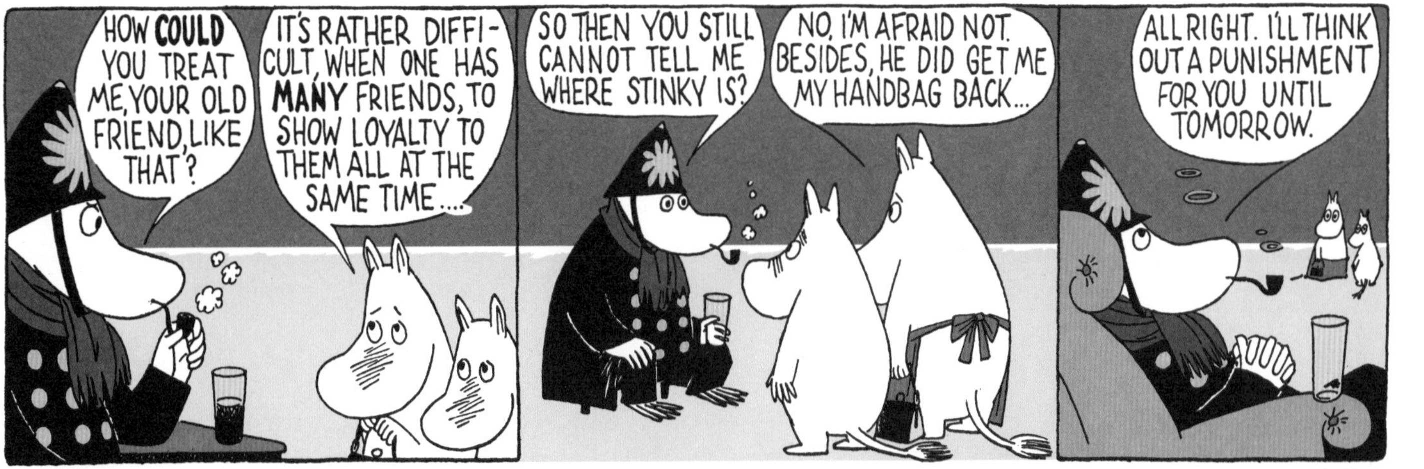
HOW **COULD** YOU TREAT ME, YOUR OLD FRIEND, LIKE THAT?
IT'S RATHER DIFFI- CULT, WHEN ONE HAS **MANY** FRIENDS, TO SHOW LOYALTY TO THEM ALL AT THE SAME TIME....
SO THEN YOU STILL CANNOT TELL ME WHERE STINKY IS?
NO, I'M AFRAID NOT. BESIDES, HE DID GET ME MY HANDBAG BACK...
ALL RIGHT. I'LL THINK OUT A PUNISHMENT FOR YOU UNTIL TOMORROW.

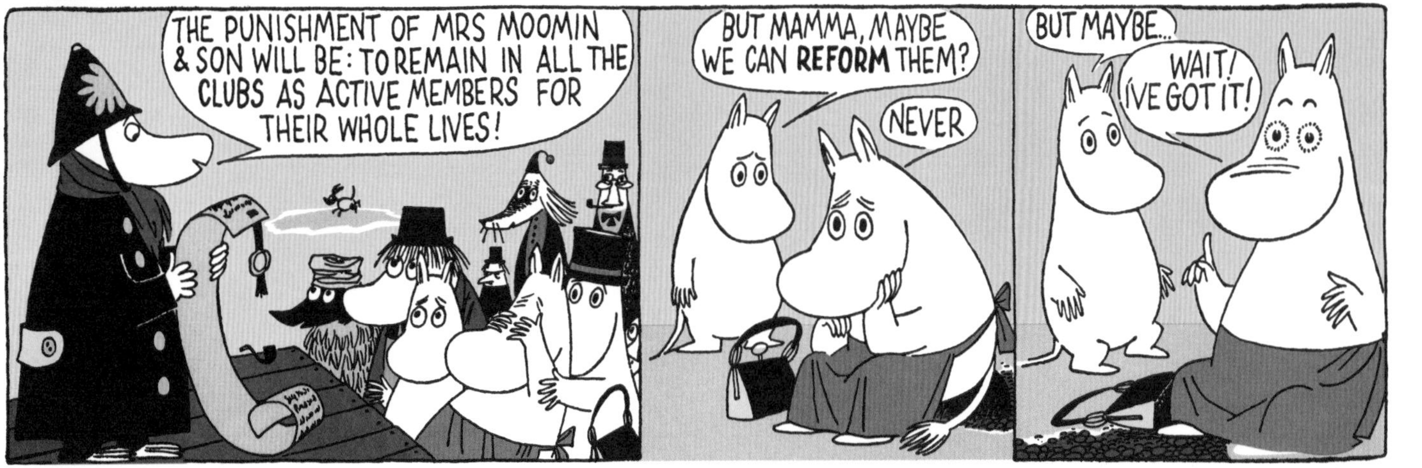
THE PUNISHMENT OF MRS MOOMIN & SON WILL BE: TO REMAIN IN ALL THE CLUBS AS ACTIVE MEMBERS FOR THEIR WHOLE LIVES!
BUT MAMMA, MAYBE WE CAN **REFORM** THEM?
NEVER
BUT MAYBE...
WAIT! I'VE GOT IT!

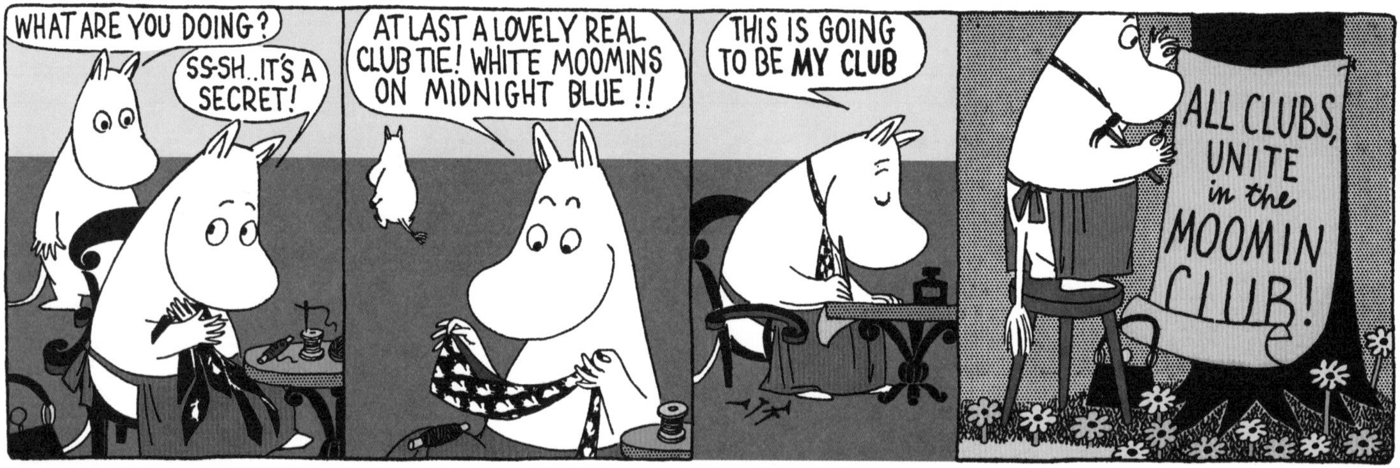
WHAT ARE YOU DOING?
SS-SH..IT'S A SECRET!
AT LAST A LOVELY REAL CLUB TIE! WHITE MOOMINS ON MIDNIGHT BLUE !!
THIS IS GOING TO BE **MY CLUB**
ALL CLUBS, UNITE in the MOOMIN CLUB!

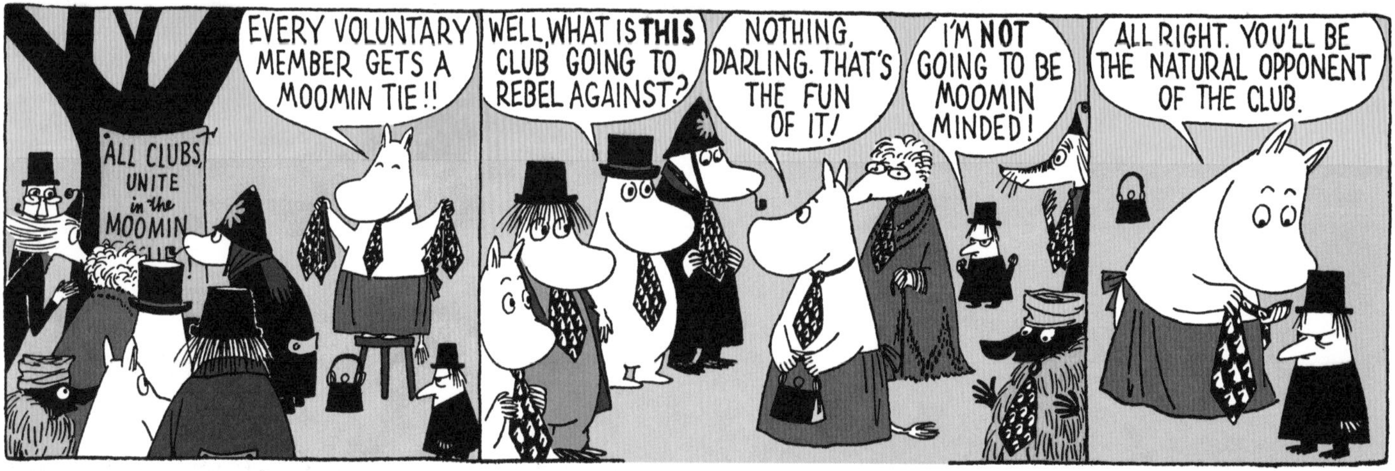
ALL CLUBS, UNITE in the MOOMIN
EVERY VOLUNTARY MEMBER GETS A MOOMIN TIE!!
WELL, WHAT IS **THIS** CLUB GOING TO REBEL AGAINST?
NOTHING, DARLING. THAT'S THE FUN OF IT!
I'M **NOT** GOING TO BE MOOMIN MINDED!
ALL RIGHT. YOU'LL BE THE NATURAL OPPONENT OF THE CLUB.

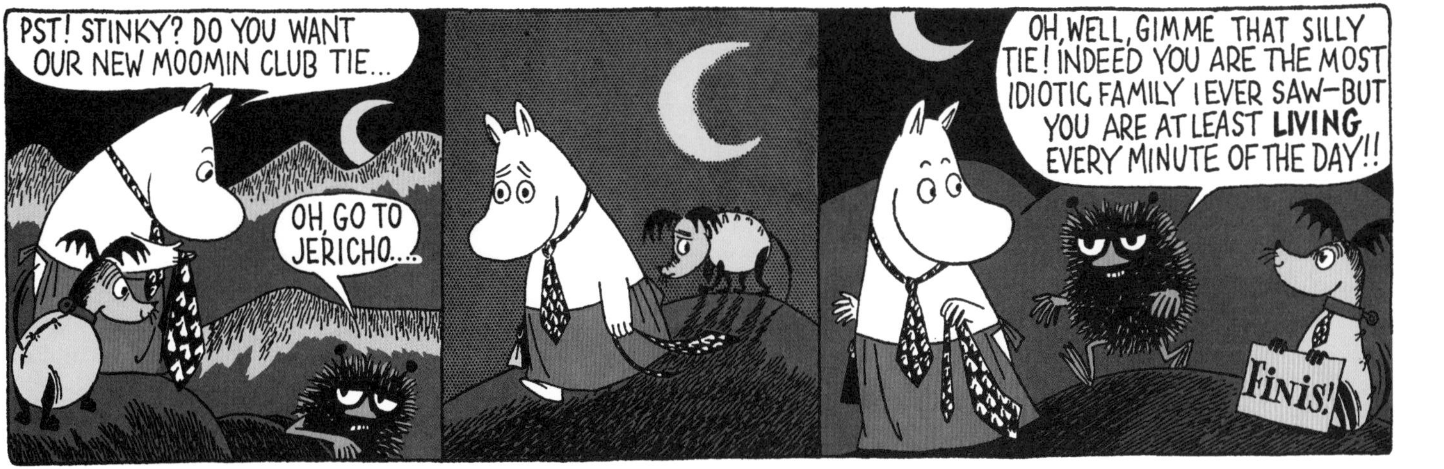
PST! STINKY? DO YOU WANT OUR NEW MOOMIN CLUB TIE...
OH, GO TO JERICHO....
OH, WELL, GIMME THAT SILLY TIE! INDEED YOU ARE THE MOST IDIOTIC FAMILY I EVER SAW—BUT YOU ARE AT LEAST **LIVING** EVERY MINUTE OF THE DAY!!
FINIS!

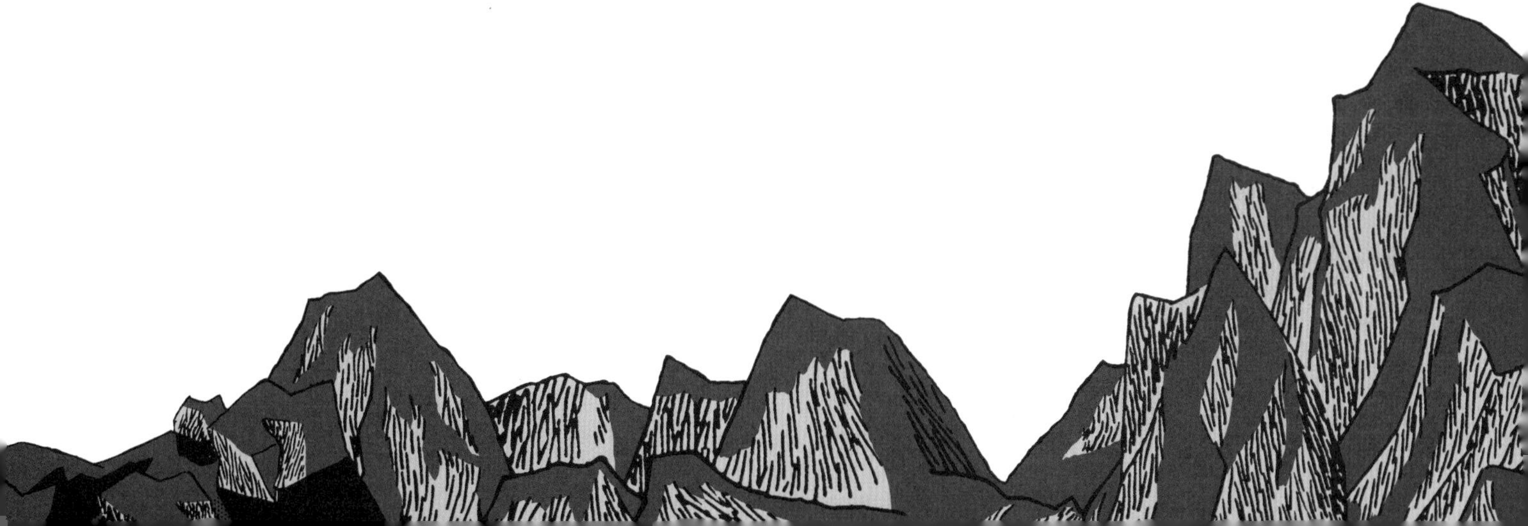

Let Enfant take you away to the exciting world of
MOOMINVALLEY! NOW IN FULL COLOR!

©SOLO/BULLS

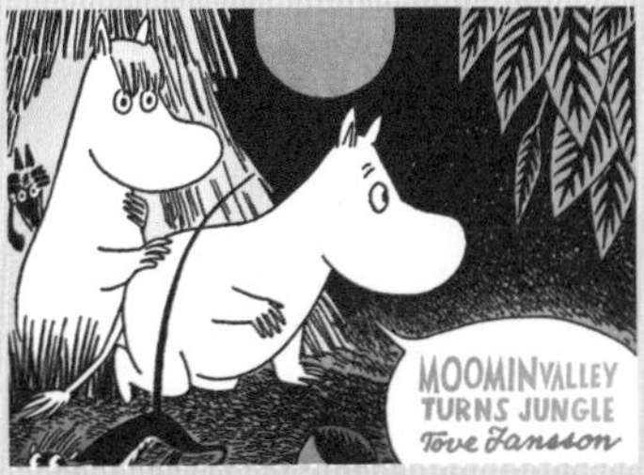
MOOMINVALLEY TURNS JUNGLE
Tove Jansson

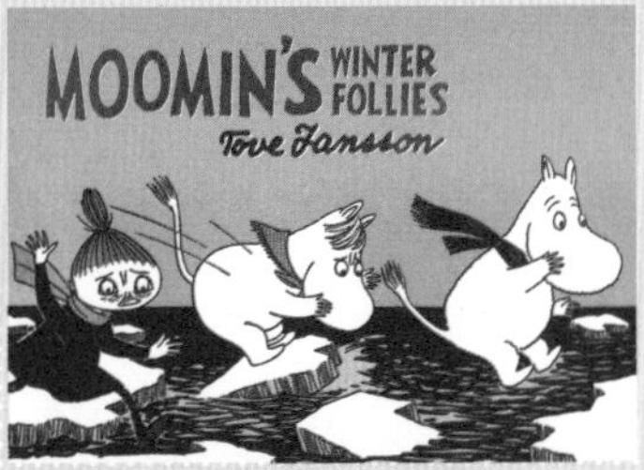
MOOMIN'S WINTER FOLLIES
Tove Jansson

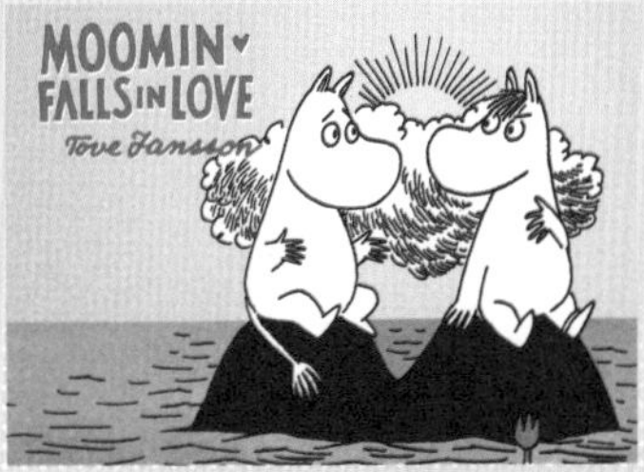
MOOMIN FALLS IN LOVE
Tove Jansson

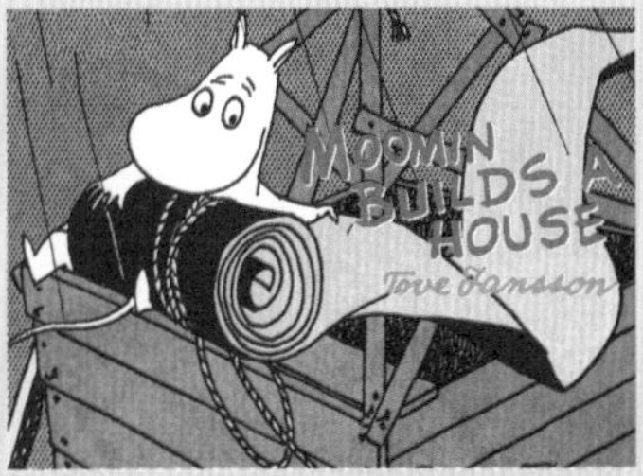
MOOMIN BUILDS A HOUSE
Tove Jansson

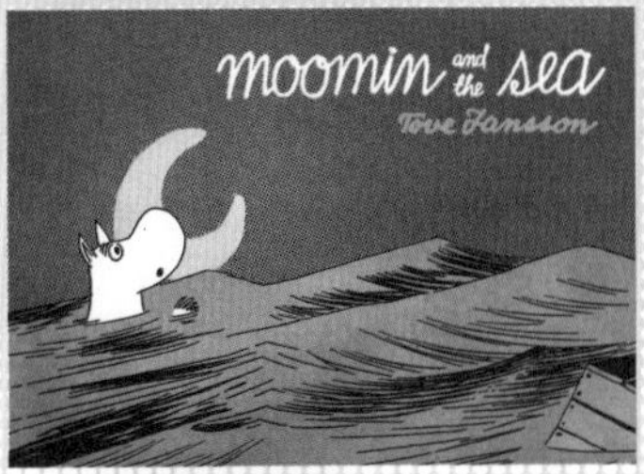
moomin and the sea
Tove Jansson

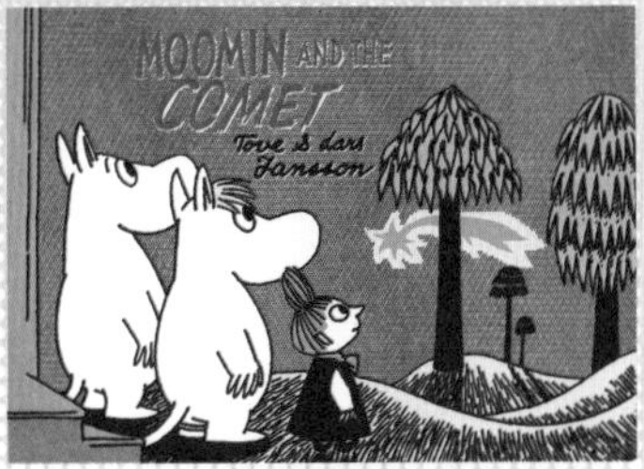
MOOMIN AND THE COMET
Tove & Lars Jansson

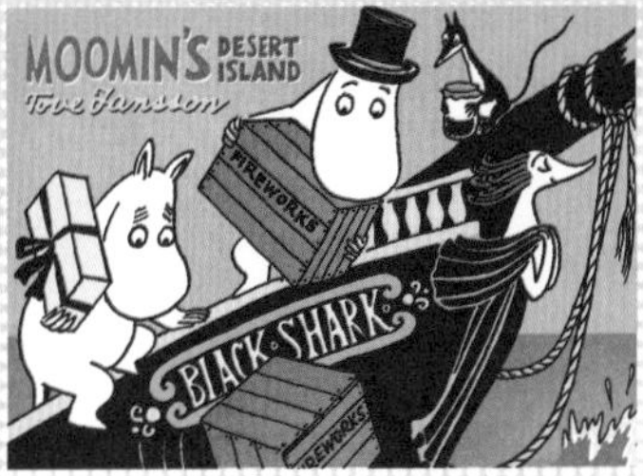
MOOMIN'S DESERT ISLAND
Tove Jansson
FIREWORKS
BLACK SHARK

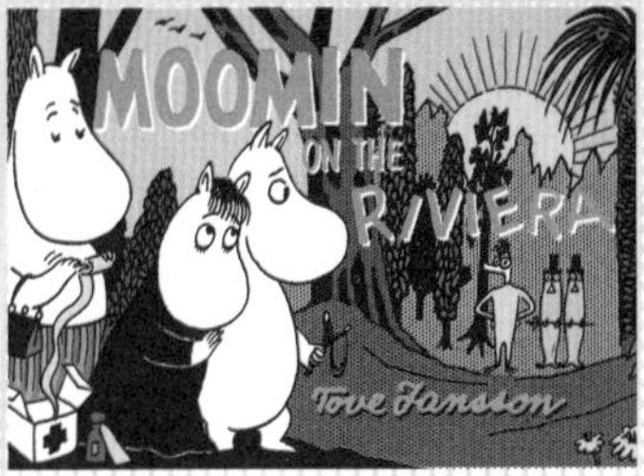
MOOMIN ON THE RIVIERA
Tove Jansson

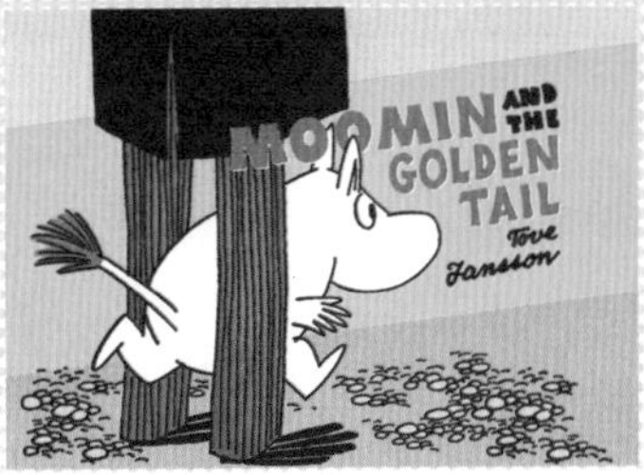
MOOMIN AND THE GOLDEN TAIL
Tove Jansson

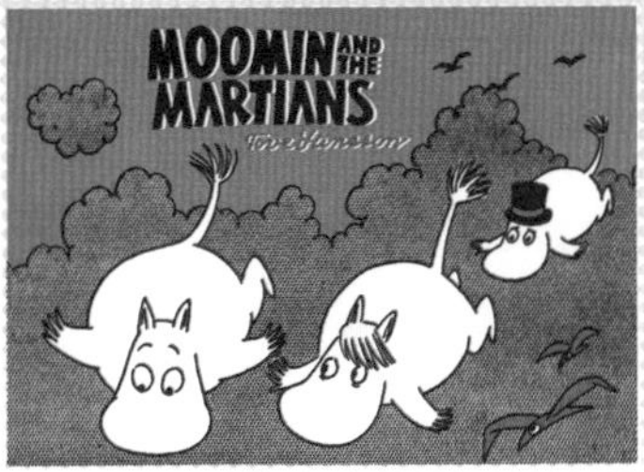
MOOMIN AND THE MARTIANS
Tove Jansson

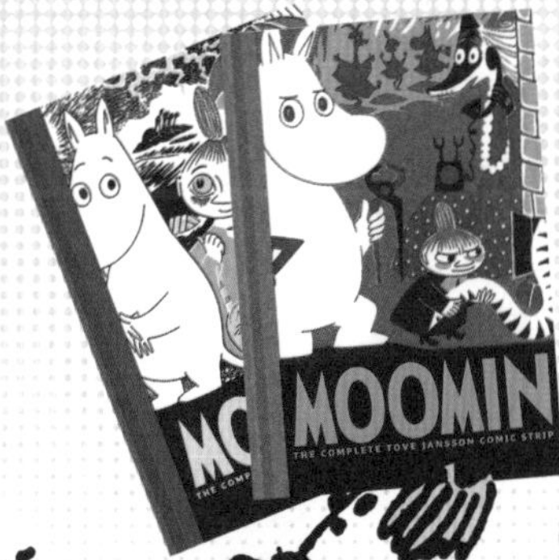
MOOMIN
THE COMPLETE TOVE JANSSON COMIC STRIP

Also available

THE TOVE AND LARS JANSSON CLASSIC HARDCOVERS

Collect the entire series, available at finer comics shops and bookstores everywhere, or from drawnandquarterly.com

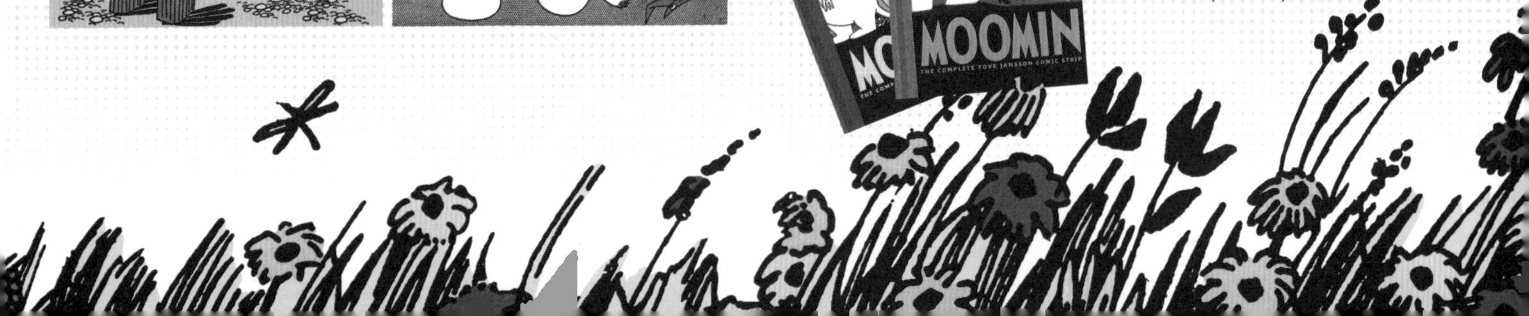

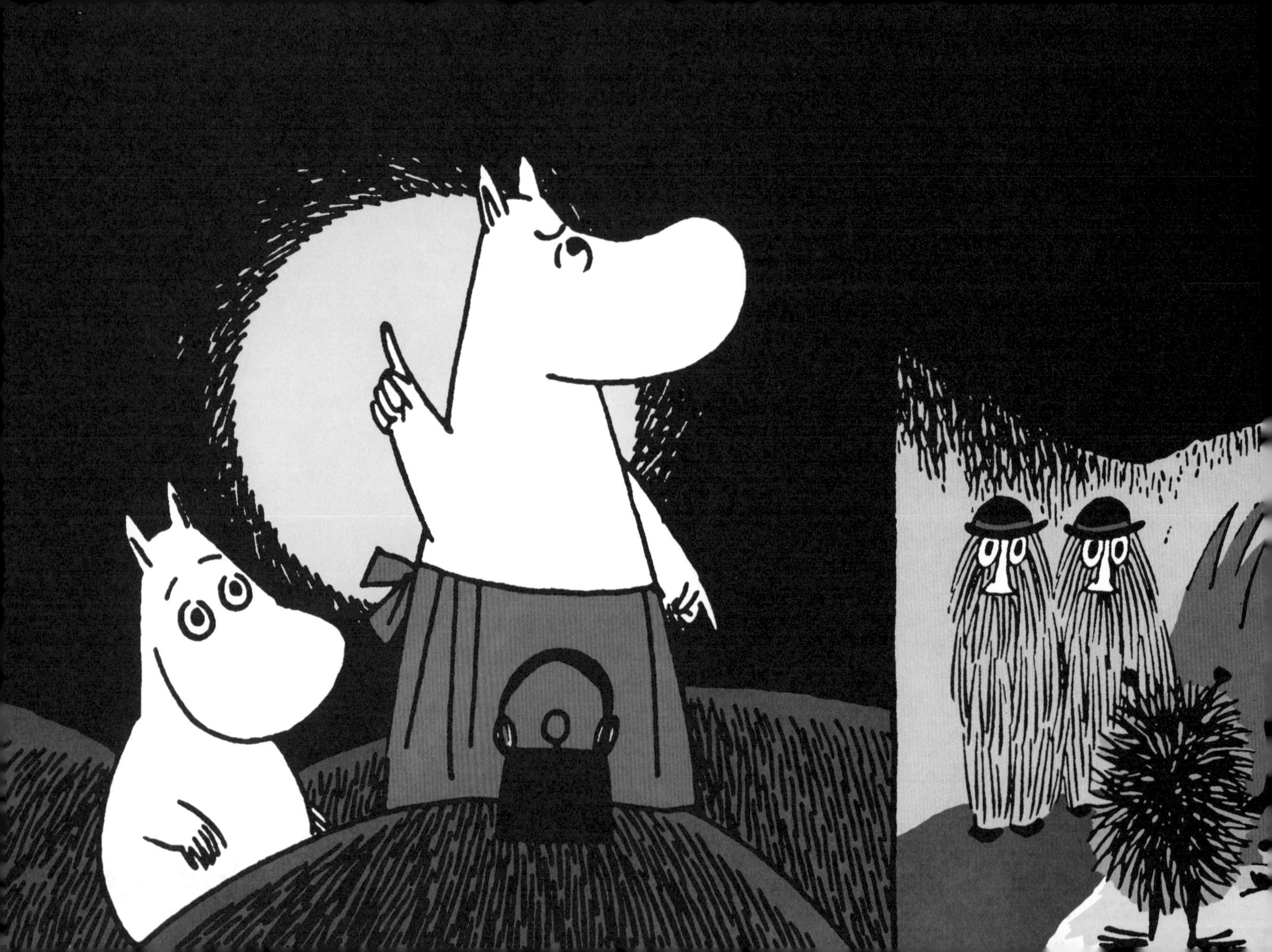

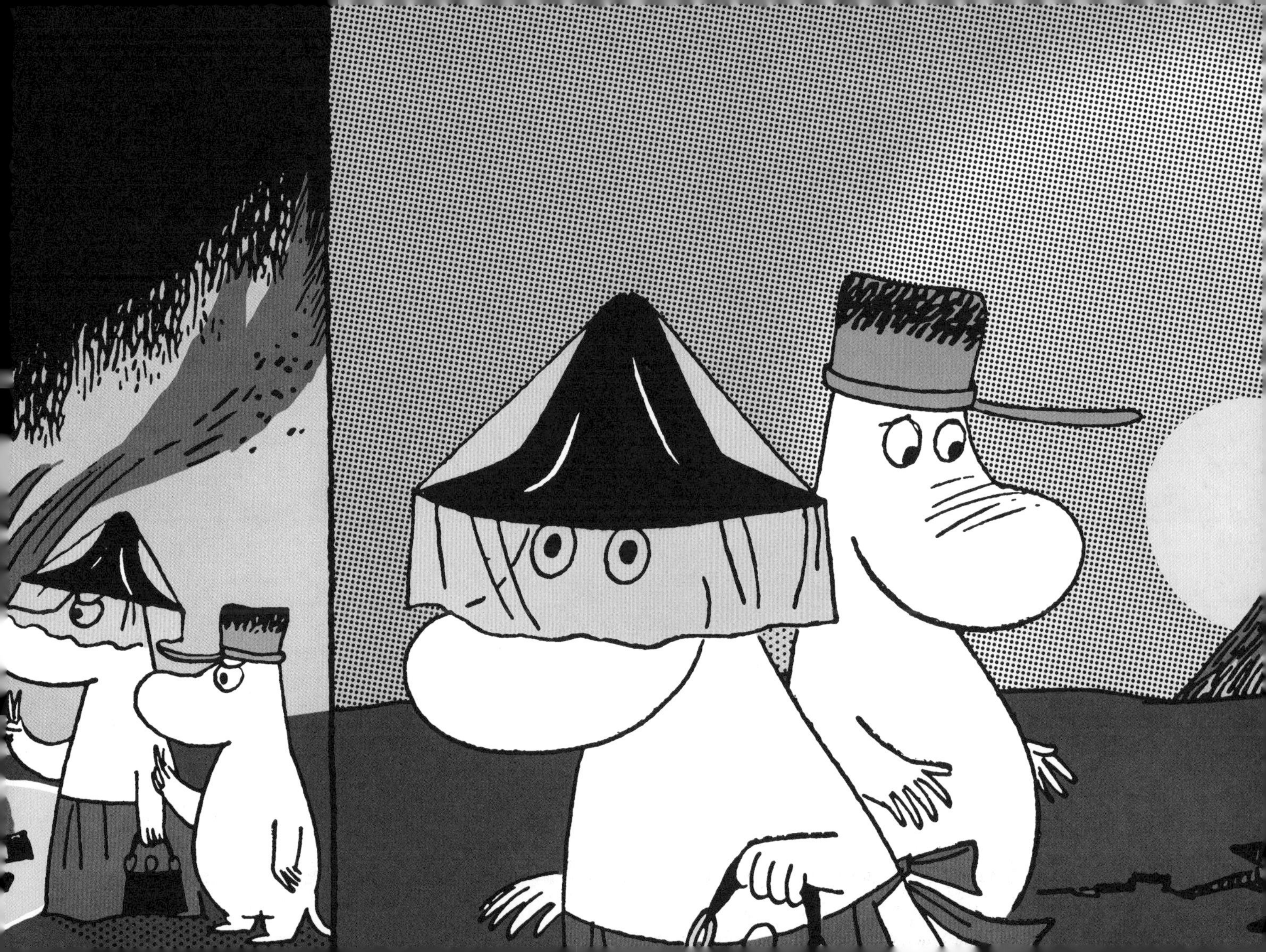

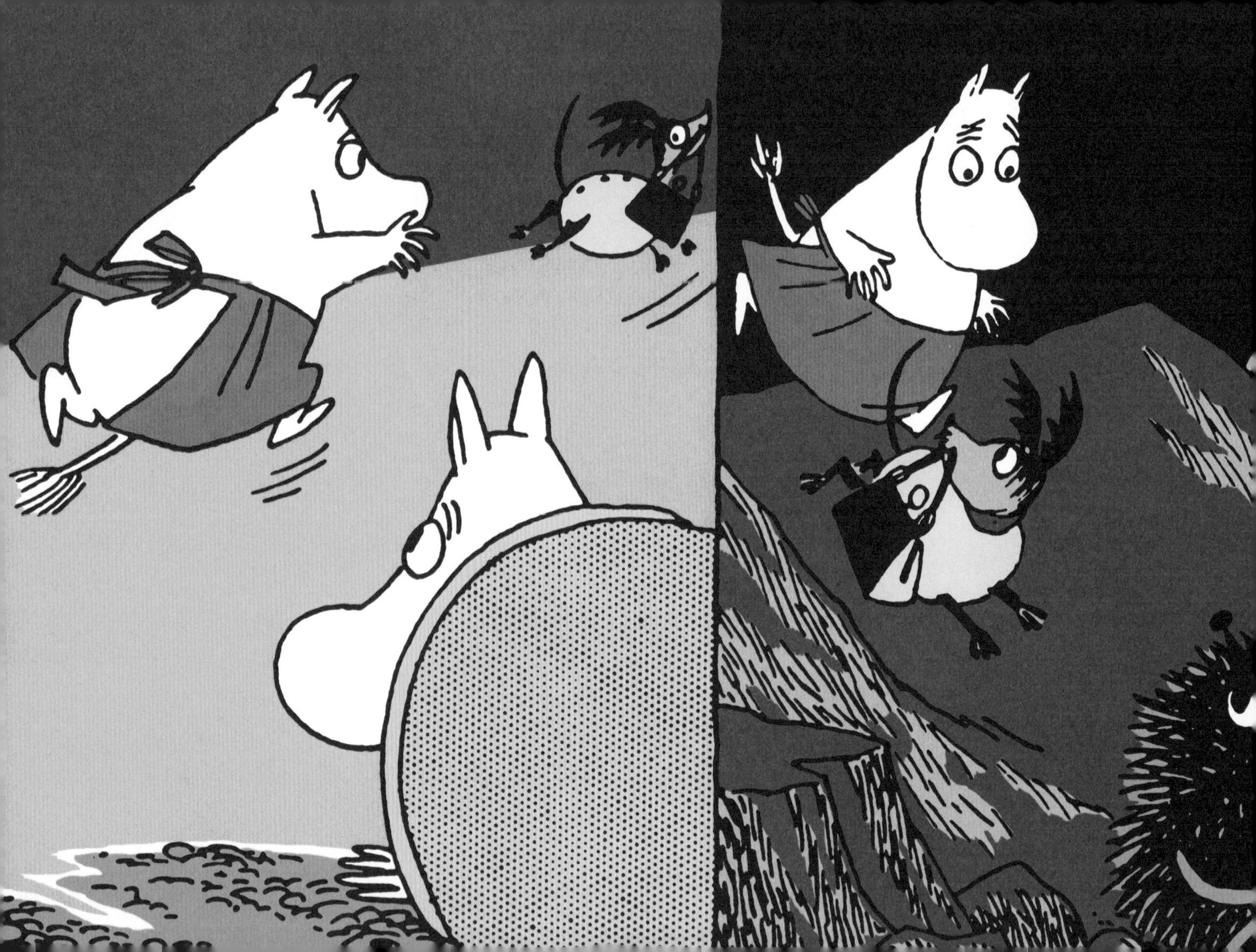

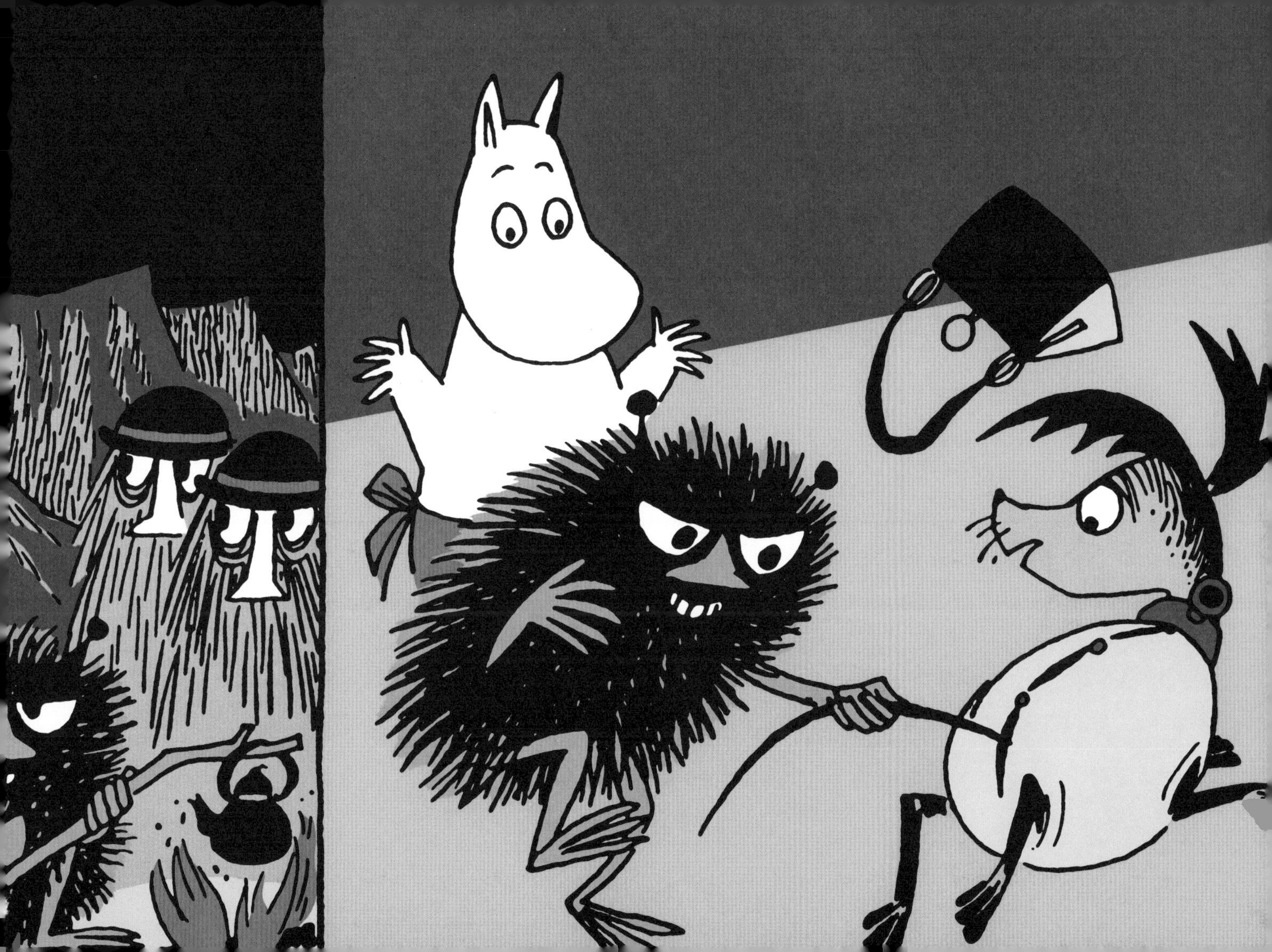

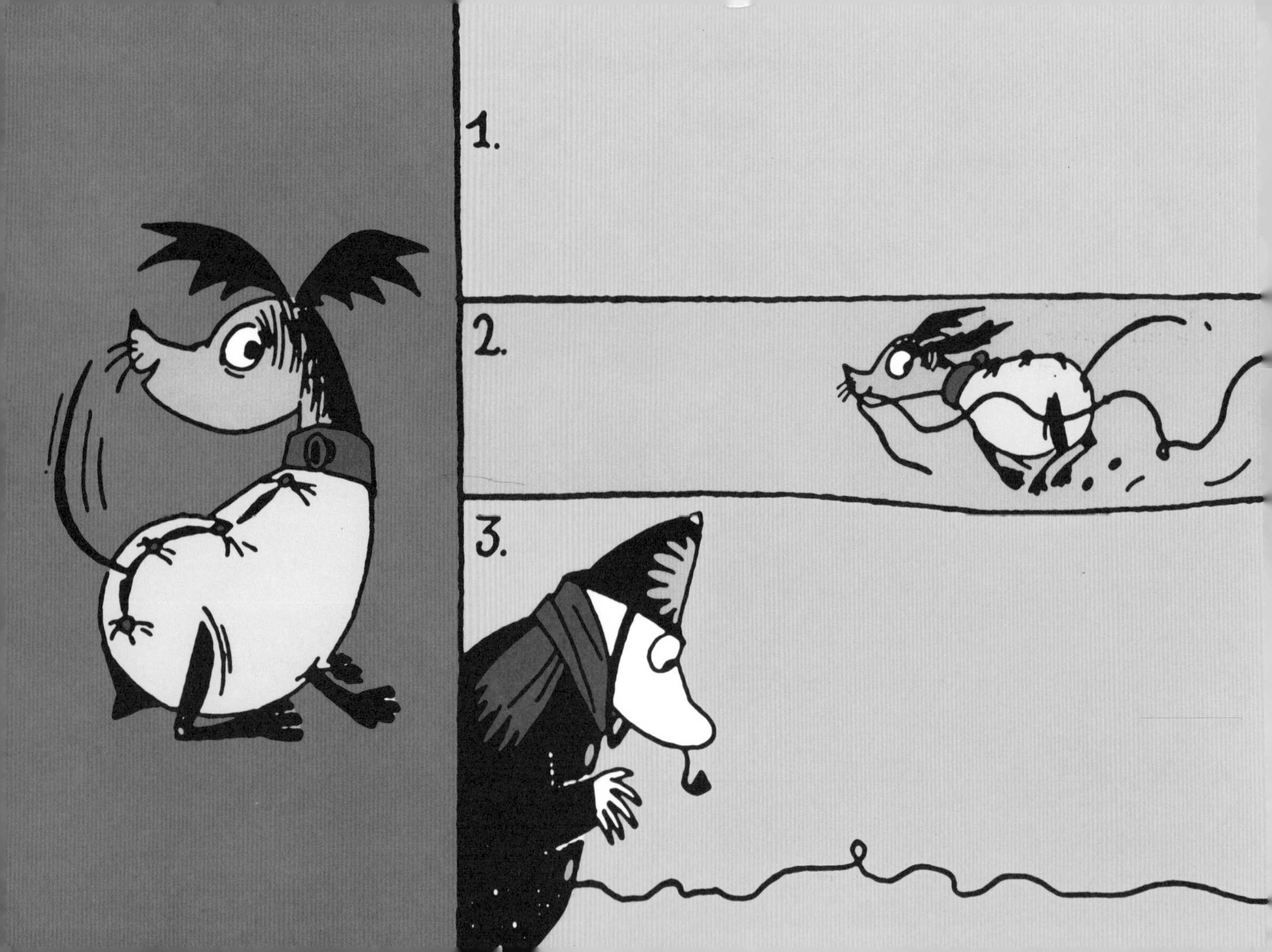
1.
2.
3.